# LINDA BUDZINSKI

*To Mom and Dad, who taught me to always be myself.*

# Em & Em

## LINDA BUDZINSKI

*Lucy —*

*You do you!* ♡

*Linda Budzinski*

# CHAPTER ONE

Ember pulled the photo from her portfolio and held it beneath the lamp on her nightstand. Though it was by far her best shot, she knew she couldn't bring it to the interview that afternoon.

She'd taken it in the spring, early in the day, with the sun hanging low over the water. Her sister's face beamed as she raced through the sea foam toward the camera, her bright pink-and-purple kite soaring high above.

They'd fought on the way to the shore that morning. Tricia complained she was too old for kites, and Ember snapped at her. "Just fly it." She needed an action shot for her photography class.

"Fine," Tricia said. "But I won't smile."

But she had smiled. A genuine, glowing, thirteen-year-old-who-still-secretly-loved-kites smile.

The shot earned an A in class and even took first place in *PhotoPro Magazine's* annual teen contest. They'd featured it on their July cover, to be admired by a million subscribers, which was precisely why Ember had to hide it now. Too much exposure. She sighed and placed it aside. She'd need to rely on the rest of her portfolio.

Ember's mom appeared in the doorway. "Ready, sweetheart? Your sister's already in the car."

She and her mother exchanged bewildered glances. Tricia had always hated school, had raised a fuss every morning as her mom struggled to get her out the door. Who would have thought that within a week of moving to Podunk, she'd become so well adjusted?

Perhaps there was a cute boy in her class. The thought made Ember uneasy. Tricia would be going to high school next year. Guy stuff got real in high school. She didn't want her sister to make the same mistakes she had.

As Ember slid into the rear seat, Tricia turned and stuck out her tongue. "Enjoy the view from the back, suckah!"

Ember mussed her hair, but only a little. It was

nice to see her sister happy. Someone should be. Tricia looked nothing like the photo now. For one thing, in the six months since it was taken, she'd grown two inches and sprouted boobs. For another, she'd had her hair cut short and darkened. Maybe now, after all they'd been through, she really was too old for kites.

Ember had dyed her own hair red—Spicy Cinnamon—to go with her new name. She was Ember O'Malley now, born and raised in Philadelphia, a transfer student with a 3.6 GPA from West Catholic High School on Chestnut Street.

Mark Twain once said that if you tell the truth, you never have to remember anything. Smart guy, that Twain. Of course, he'd never been in Witness Protection. That tended to complicate things.

The GPA was true. As for the rest? Well, she wasn't Irish, not even a little bit. She was Polish, mostly, with a little German and Norwegian thrown in on her mom's side. And she'd never even set foot in the City of Brotherly Love.

The ride to school took a half hour despite the fact that there was zero traffic. All week long, Ember had ridden with her eyes closed, listening to her iPod, trying to block everything out. Especially that night. The roar of the surf, the harsh taste of tequila, the stench of vomit, and most of all, the sickly blue tinge of the dead girl's lips. She rarely succeeded. No music was loud enough to make all that go away.

Today, though, Ember left her iPod in her backpack. She needed to prepare for her interview with the *Bruins Bulletin*. She was sure it would be the lamest school newspaper in the world, but she was still nervous. She didn't merely *want* this photography position, she *needed* it. She needed something to hold onto. Something familiar to keep her grounded.

She unzipped the inside pocket of her backpack. There, beneath the lining, hid a secret compartment with her cheat sheet. She took out the sheet and unfolded it. She'd been over it a hundred times, but sometimes, especially when she was nervous, she'd forget the details. And she'd ramble. Forgetting and rambling were a bad combination.

"You'll do fine, Em." Her mom eyed her in the rearview mirror. She tried to sound casual, but Ember could tell she was worried too.

"They're going to ask a lot of questions. What if I screw up?"

"Your photos are beautiful. That's all they need to know. They don't need to ask questions."

"Mom, it's an interview. They'll ask questions."

The straight A's in her digital photo classes, the top photography position on her school's yearbook staff, the first-place prize in the annual district-wide art show—that was all true. It was when, where, and with whom that tripped her up.

"Oh, crap."

Her mom and Tricia both looked back at her. "What's wrong?" her mom asked.

"The yearbook. What if they ask to see it?"

"Tell them you forgot it," Tricia said.

"What if they ask me to bring it in tomorrow?"

Her sister shrugged. "Tell them it was destroyed in a massive fire."

"A fire." Ember sighed. She almost wished it were that simple. She'd have to leave it off her application. Too risky. She crammed the cheat sheet back into its compartment. Her mom was right. Her best bet was to let her portfolio do the talking. Keep her answers short, sweet, and as devoid of details as possible.

She rested her head back and tried to distract herself for the rest of the ride by counting silos. She'd hoped that moving to the Midwest would be like dropping onto the set of *Downton Abbey*, minus the abbey. Quaint cottages, rolling green pastures, an occasional sheep. But Boyd County was nothing like the English countryside. It consisted of one endless field after another—corn and wheat and alfalfa, whatever that was—huge expanses of brown punctuated by the occasional red barn. More cows lived here than people, and it smelled like it too. It had a pungent, earthy smell that was nothing at all like the salt air she was used to.

What would Zach think if he were here? Ember's insides ached at the thought. It had only been a week since she'd left, but she missed him so much—his loose dark curls, the way his broad shoulders strained against his favorite Mets jersey, the way he stroked her hair when they kissed. If only Ember could call him or text him. If only she'd had a chance to say goodbye, to explain what she was doing and why.

She blinked back tears as they pulled up to the high school. She had to keep herself together, especially today.

"Good luck," her mom said. "With the interview and … everything."

"Yeah, good luck." Her sister smirked. "Don't say anything that'll get us all killed."

# CHAPTER TWO

Ember snatched a copy of the *Bruins Bulletin* off the rack by the front door. It came out on Fridays, so this was the first edition she'd ever actually seen. The front page featured a story on school repairs, with a photo of a janitor high atop a ladder changing a light bulb. The tilted angle gave the illusion that the janitor might fall, adding a brilliant sense of tension to what could have been a boring shot.

She checked the photo credit. *M.L. Martin.* Whoever M.L. Martin was, he knew what he was doing. Crap.

Ember hugged her portfolio to her chest and headed to her first class, AP History. Slipping into a seat in the back row, she opened the paper. A bunch of 4-H Club awards, five pages of football coverage, a profile of one of the shop teachers—lame, lame, lame—though Ember had to admit, the writing was good. And the photos were even better.

"What was it like?"

Ember looked up to find a blond, blue-eyed, corn-fed girl in a red-and-white cheerleading uniform sitting next to her. She glanced around to see whether the girl might be talking to someone else, but it was six minutes before the first bell and they were alone. "What was what like?"

"Living in the city. In Philadelphia." The girl's eyes were as wide around as the silos Ember had been counting.

Ember shrugged. "I don't know. It was … a big place, with lots of people." She turned back to the paper, hoping the girl would go away.

No such luck.

"I'm Claire." She leaned into the aisle and dropped her voice. "You must have been so pissed at your parents for moving here."

"Actually, it's just my mom. She and my dad split up a long time ago." Ember left it at that. The less said the better, and anyway, no one had been able to dream up a decent story for why they were here. They had no friends or relatives for a thousand miles—that was kind of the point—and the job market in this part of the country wasn't exactly booming.

"I can't wait to get out of this place," Claire said. "I want to go to NYU. For theater."

"Theater?" Ember never would have pegged her as a drama geek.

"Yep. I'm counting the days. It's … " Claire paused, her lips moving as she did a quick calculation. "It's 697 days from now."

Ember smiled. Maybe she was a geek. A fresh-faced, rah-rah, "Give Me a B" type of geek, but a geek nonetheless.

"What about you?" Claire asked. "You probably want to get back to the East Coast, like, yesterday, right? Where do you think you'll go to school?"

"I don't know. Maybe Long Island U." The photography program there was one of the best.

"Long Island?" Claire clasped her perfectly manicured hands together. "That sounds awesome. And it's probably not too far from NYU, right? So I'll know somebody out there."

"I guess." Ember turned back to her paper. "But 697 days is a long time. Who knows what'll happen between now and then?" She shifted in her seat, making it clear the conversation was over.

This time Claire took the hint and stood. "Guess

I'll see you around … " Her voice trailed off as she drifted away, toward her seat at the front of the room.

Ember kept her head down, eyes on the paper. She had no girlfriends back home, and she didn't need one here. Keep a low profile and stay out of trouble. That was the plan, and if everything worked out, she'd be back in Jersey in a few months. She'd go home and testify, justice would be served, and she and Zach could go on as though none of this had ever happened.

Deputy Steuben and her mom had warned her not to get her hopes up. They said things didn't always work out that way. They said she could end up spending her last two years of high school in Witness Protection, maybe longer, maybe even forever. But they were wrong. They had to be.

The morning dragged by. Ember was already behind, since they started school two weeks earlier here than back in Jersey. She tried to concentrate in her classes, but all she could think about was her interview. At lunch, she grabbed a grilled cheese sandwich and searched for an empty table. Lunch was the worst part of her day. She could feel the other kids staring as she ate. It wasn't that they were being mean or threatening, but she had a feeling they didn't get too many new kids here. Avoiding eye contact, she made a beeline toward the back of the room, until a shout stopped her.

"Ember!" It was Claire, waving and walking toward her. "Come sit with us."

Ember muttered an excuse about needing to study for a quiz, but it was no use. Claire steered her toward a table of six girls. All cheerleaders. Fantastic.

"Everyone, this is Ember. Ember, this is… everyone."

"Everyone who matters," one girl said.

Ember could swear she saw Claire roll her eyes. "Nice meeting you." She stood awkwardly, balancing her tray, backpack, and portfolio.

"Sit." One of the girls swiped a backpack off the chair next to her and pointed.

"Thanks." As she sat down, she could feel them watching, sizing her up. She was glad she'd let her mom talk her into toning things down here. She'd penciled on a little less eyeliner than she wore back home, sported a cami under her shirt to cover up her cleavage, and lost her ever-present silver mermaid ear cuff. If anyone looked closely enough, they might have wondered why she had three tiny tan lines circling the cartilage of her right ear.

"Ember's from Philadelphia," Claire said. "And she's going to college at Long Island."

The Everyone-Who-Matters girl offered up a smile that hinted at a sneer. "Claire's obsessed with New York. Bright lights, big city, and all that. Thinks she's *too cool for country.*" She added an exaggerated twang to that last part.

This time Claire's eye roll was unmistakable. "Give me a break, Marissa. Where else is a theater major supposed to go?" She looked around at her friends. "Who remembers the last time a Broadway show came to Boyd County? Anyone? Anyone? No? Oh, right, because that was … never."

Ember couldn't help but laugh.

Marissa arched a meticulously plucked eyebrow. "We're not a bunch of hicks, you know. We may not have skyscrapers and traffic and … " She waved a hand in the air, trying to think of one other thing a major metropolis might have that her cow-infested county did not.

"A decent coffee shop?" Ember offered. It was one of the things she missed most since she'd arrived. Besides the shore. And Zach.

"We have a Starbucks inside the grocery," Marissa muttered, but it was obvious the way she and the other girls shifted in their seats that they all knew how lame that sounded.

Claire spoke up. "So. Big game tonight!" Her voice was a little too bright, but the change of subject worked. Ember gave her a grateful smile as the girls' conversation took off into a barrage of plans for pre-game warm ups and post-game parties. Ember nibbled at her sandwich and studied them. Their hair, their makeup, the way they dressed, and the stuff they talked about—they were different from the girls back home, but also the same. She tried to imagine what would have happened if she'd tried to sit down at a table full of cheerleaders at her old high school. Impossible.

When the bell rang, Ember grabbed her stuff to take off. She suspected she wouldn't have to worry about Claire ever talking to her again, but she was mistaken. Claire appeared at her side. "Tonight should be fun. Ewing High is our biggest rival. You're coming, right?"

Ember stared at her. The girl was persistent, she had to give her that. And she seemed sincere, like she honestly wanted to be friends. Of course, she didn't know a thing about who Ember really was—the things she'd seen, the things she'd done.

Something Ember's mom had said on the plane ride here whispered to her, tempted her: *This could be a new beginning, a fresh start for all of us.*

Ember pushed the thought away. This was nothing of the sort. It was a temporary escape, a safe haven until she did what she had to do. Besides, people couldn't run away from their true selves.

"Please say you're coming," Claire repeated.

Ember shook her head. "I can't make it. I need to finish unpacking."

It was a lie. She, her mom, and her sister had brought only a few suitcases. They hadn't had time to grab more than that. Truth was, she planned to spend the evening doing what she'd done every night since they'd arrived: obsessively checking Zach's Facebook, Twitter, and Instagram accounts. It was pathetic, yes, but it would be better than standing in the freezing cold cheering on some stupid team she didn't care about. She despised high school football. Or, to be more precise, high school football players.

# CHAPTER THREE

*One year earlier*

Jimmy: Hey, Slutkowski, nice video. I'm impressed.

Emily read the cryptic message three times before closing her phone. What was Jimmy d'Angelo talking about? What video? She lifted her throbbing head and tried to focus. The last thing she remembered was jumping into the hot tub with Jimmy and his friend, Brad.

"Hey, Moll." She shook her friend, who was passed out next to her. "Moll, wake up."

Molly rolled over and groaned. "Go away."

Emily shook her again. "Come on. This is important. I need to know what happened last night."

Molly pulled her comforter over her head. "I had a

party. It was epic."

"Yes. It was. But do you remember anything about a video?"

Molly peeked out. "Video?"

"Yeah. Look." Emily held her phone up. "A text from Jimmy."

"Idiot." Molly said Jimmy put the "offensive" in offensive line. She said he was a loser and an egomaniac and half his family was made up of Mafia thugs. "If the video is from last night, it's probably not pretty."

Somewhere in the back of Emily's mind, a small alarm began to ring. Between that dip in the hot tub and waking up on Molly's bed, what had happened? She wasn't sure. Her head fell back onto the pillow. She thought she'd cut herself off after her second Jell-O shot, but she must have had more. Why was her mind such a fog? "Did I sing? Please don't tell me I sang. Or danced."

But Molly had already fallen back asleep.

Emily tapped her phone. Maybe the video was on Facebook or Twitter or YouTube. She searched with no luck. Maybe Jimmy was just messing with her. She closed her eyes and replayed the night—or as much as she could remember of it—in her head.

She and most everyone else had arrived at Molly's at ten o'clock, right after the football game. The first person she saw when she walked through the door was Zach Reagan. Zach was shy, the school's all-star pitcher, and he could carve a wave like no one else. She'd been crushing on him forever, so she about died when he handed her the first Jell-O shot of the night.

She downed it without ever taking her eyes off his. It was cool and sweet and burned her throat just a teeny bit on the way down. "Thanks," she said. "I'm Emily. We have lunch together. I mean, the same period. Not that we sit together or anything."

Zach gave her an odd look, and Emily felt her face grow red. She turned, fake-waved to someone across the room, and escaped. Total flirting fail.

She spotted Jimmy and Brad standing in a corner. They both still wore their eye black—as if they'd needed it for a night game. She and Jimmy sat next to each other in geometry. He flirted with her sometimes, though she couldn't tell whether it was because he liked her or because he wanted to cheat off her homework. Jimmy had muscles on top of muscles, a hot car, and a never-ending stream of girls drooling after him. Emily glanced back. Zach was still watching her. Oh, man. She had to talk to someone. She took a deep breath and walked up to Jimmy and Brad.

"Hey, guys. Good game." They'd lost, twenty-eight to three.

Brad scowled, but Jimmy gave her a huge smile. "Hey, Em. Thanks." He turned to Brad. "This chick really knows her angles. Isosceles triangles and trapezoids and all that stuff." He was slurring his words. "But you know what I like most about her?" He leaned toward Brad and whispered loud enough so Emily could hear. "I like her curves."

Emily blushed and laughed. She glanced back toward where Zach had been standing. He was gone, probably hooking up with someone much less dorky than her.

"Hey, where's your drink?" Jimmy asked. He shouted to no one in particular. "Get this girl some Jell-O shots!"

Things started to blur after that. There was another shot, a game of poker, which Emily lost, a game of I Never, which she won by a landslide, and finally the hot tub. Emily had borrowed one of Molly's bikinis, and she remembered constantly having to tug at the bra because her chest was smaller than Molly's.

That was it. She didn't remember getting out of the hot tub, Jimmy and Brad leaving, crawling into bed, none of that. And she certainly didn't remember anyone shooting videos.

She had just resigned herself to calling Jimmy and asking him what he was talking about when her phone rang. It was him.

"What video?"

"Well, good morning, Miss Sunshine," he said. "You know what video. You were waving at the camera."

The alarm in Emily's head returned, louder. Much louder. "I swear, I have no idea what you're talking about."

Jimmy laughed. "It's on the way." He hung up.

A few minutes later, Emily's phone buzzed. She checked her text, and there it was—a three-second GIF of her in the hot tub with the entire offensive line. She was topless, dangling Molly's bikini bra in the air and, as Jimmy had said, smiling and waving at the camera. The GIF played over and over and over, until at last Emily threw her phone across the room. She ran into Molly's bathroom and puked.

# CHAPTER FOUR

Clutching her portfolio, Ember wound through a crowded maze of desks, computers, and newspaper stacks toward a cubicle in the back of Room 221, home of the *Bruins Bulletin*. A sign taped to the side of the cubicle read, "Editor in Chief: Charles Moore."

She paused and cleared her throat. "Hello?"

No answer.

"Hello? I'm here for the interview?"

A rustling noise from behind made her jump. Ember turned to face a guy who was slightly taller than her. He had a dark mop of hair poking out at interesting angles, a lightly stubbled chin, and intense brown eyes framed by thick-rimmed glasses.

"Hello. I'm Charles." His voice was deep and warm. He held out his hand, and she nearly dropped her portfolio as she reached out to shake it. "Sorry. Let me take that for you." He set her portfolio on the nearest desk and gave an appreciative nod. "Old school."

Ember's face grew warm. "I know. It's just … photos can look so different in print." She unzipped her backpack and pulled out a jump drive. "I brought this, too, though. So you can scroll through them on the screen if it's easier."

But Charles had already opened her portfolio and was bent over it. He didn't say a word, merely nodded as he examined each shot.

Ember was proud of her photos and loved sharing them, but Charles's intensity as he pored over them made her feel self-conscious. She'd weeded out the ones that showed the name of her old school or too much of her hometown, but still, these were her closest connection to her past, to everything she'd left behind.

She tried to read his expression. Did he like them? Hate them? His face revealed nothing.

"So, do you go by Charlie? Chuck? Chaz?"

"No." He shook his head, never taking his eyes from the photos. "It's Charles." He said it just like that. As though it were the most natural thing in the world for a teenage boy living in the United States of

America to call himself Charles.

"Oh. Well, I'm Ember. Or Em. Either one."

Charles straightened. "I'm sorry. I'm being rude. Please sit." He pointed to a nearby desk and sat down across from her.

It wasn't until Ember sank into the chair that she realized how badly her knees had been shaking. She took a deep breath. "I realize you're already almost a month into the school year, but if there's any way at all I could—"

"We need a photographer."

"You do?"

Charles nodded. "We have one, and she's excellent, but she can't shoot the football games. We need somebody to work the games."

Ember forced a smile. Football? Not exactly what she'd had in mind. She pointed to a *Bulletin* on the desk beside her. "So this other photographer. She took that picture of the janitor?"

"Yep. Brilliant angle, isn't it? And look at this shot from last week." Charles leafed through a stack of papers on a nearby rack and pulled one out. Its cover had a huge close-up of a volcano erupting. It wasn't a real volcano, of course. It was someone's science project, but the lighting in the photo made it appear like something straight out of Hawaii.

So M.L. Martin was a she, and the janitor shot was no fluke.

Staring at the volcano, Ember felt as though her head might explode. This interview wasn't going at all the way she'd imagined. Her biggest fear had been tripping over a detail about her "past." She hadn't even considered that the *Bulletin* might have someone on staff as good as—maybe even better than—her. Someone who could make the banal so … beautiful. "School repairs and science fairs. Amazing."

Charles's eyes narrowed. "What do you mean by that?"

"Nothing, it's just … I'm impressed."

"Right." He stood. "I realize you probably had more interesting stories than broken light fixtures where you came from, but just because we don't have stabbings and drug busts every week doesn't mean we don't put out a solid paper."

Ember stared down at her hands. She'd given the wrong impression. Sort of. Just this morning, she'd been thinking about how lame the paper would be, but now, seeing these amazing photos and listening to Charles, she wanted to take it all back. Still, he had no right to assume anything about where she came from, even if she didn't really come from there. She met his gaze. "The metal detectors cut way down on the stabbings, you know."

Now it was his turn to appear uncomfortable. "I wasn't ... I didn't mean to—"

Ember sighed and stood to face him. "Forget it. You need someone to shoot the games? I can do that. Just tell me when and where."

She didn't need to be friends with Charles. She didn't even need to get along with him. In fact, the last thing she needed was this oddly cute boy in her life to complicate things.

Charles walked over to a huge calendar of the school year hanging on the wall. "I know it's short notice, but can you start tonight?"

Ember hesitated. She almost felt as though she'd be cheating on Zach if she didn't spend her Friday night stalking him. But that was ridiculous, right? Plus, she couldn't very well turn down her first assignment. "Sure. No problem."

Charles disappeared into his cubicle and returned with a press pass. "This will give you full field access."

"Awesome." Full field access. Allowing her to stand on the sidelines right alongside the players— Midwestern versions of Jimmy and Brad. Up close and personal.

"Something wrong?" Charles asked.

"No. Not at all." Ember took a deep breath. She

was being a brat. She'd wanted a spot on the paper, and he was giving her one. She should be grateful. "I've got this. Thanks."

She reached for her portfolio, but Charles stopped her. "Who is this?" He pointed to a photo of Zach on the mound. She'd shot it during one of his practices. She loved the way his arm extended in one direction and his leg in the other as he released the ball, creating an odd combination of tension and balance. And, of course, there were his muscles. His beautiful, tanned muscles.

Ember could feel Charles's eyes on her as he waited for her answer. "He's a friend from back home." Her voice cracked as she said it, but Charles let it go.

"It's a great shot."

"Thanks." Ember closed the portfolio and headed toward the door.

"You know, it's funny," Charles called after her, and she stopped and turned. "Your friend is wearing a Mets jersey in that photo. I'd always heard Philly fans were so loyal."

Ember forced a laugh. "Yeah, well, he always was a rebel." She gave an awkward wave and shot out of the classroom, down the hallway, and out the front door. She didn't stop to breathe until she reached her mom's waiting car.

"Are you okay, sweetie?" her mom asked. "How did the interview go?"

"Fine. It went fine. Great, in fact." Ember gave her mom what she hoped was a reassuring smile.

It was true. She was the *Bruins Bulletin's* newest photographer. And Charles's comment about Zach's jersey was merely an observation. No way did he suspect anything. He couldn't possibly.

# CHAPTER FIVE

Where had all these people come from? Ember scanned the stands. The entire county, not to mention all of Ewing, had to be here. Now she understood the five pages of coverage in the school paper. And also how much trust Charles had placed in her with this assignment.

She shivered and zipped up her jacket. It was a chilly night for September, and an angry wind whipped around the field. She'd much rather be home in her warm bedroom, or better yet, back in Jersey in Zach's arms.

A cannon blast heralded the Bruins' arrival onto the field. All forty-two of them charged past, a herd of two-legged beasts shouting and grunting and slapping each other's backsides. Ember ducked into the shadows of the bleachers and stroked the rim of her camera lens, feeling the rough plastic ridges against her fingertips. She could do this.

Her camera. It felt so natural draped around her neck. It was a part of her, like another limb, or more accurately, another eye. It was as though the simple act of carrying it somehow brought the world into sharper focus. She hadn't taken a photo in nearly three weeks, since before all the trouble, and she hadn't realized until now how much she'd missed it.

Once the stampede ended, she ventured back out onto the sidelines and searched the stands for her mom and Tricia. They'd insisted on coming, and though Ember had protested, in a way she was glad they were here. A waving motion caught her attention, and she recognized her mom's slim figure and long dark hair. Tricia, almost as tall as her mom now, stood beside her, smiling down at Ember but apparently too cool to wave. Ember grinned and stuck out her tongue.

"Nice lens." A Bruins player appeared beside her.

Ember started, biting her tongue. "Ouch!"

"Sorry. Are you okay?" His voice sounded familiar, but she couldn't make out his face under the helmet. He reached toward her, but Ember shrunk back.

"I'm fine."

The player took off his helmet. Ember blinked. "Charles?" He wasn't wearing his glasses. She wasn't sure whether he looked better with or without them, and she had a sudden vision of Clark Kent transforming himself from nerdy reporter into a caped football superhero. "You? Play football?"

"Yes. Why is that so hard to believe?" He looked down at the ground. "I'm the place kicker."

Crap. For the second time today Charles thought she was dissing him. It wasn't that she couldn't imagine him playing, it was just … seriously? Did every male above the age of seven here have to suit up? "I'm sorry," she said. "I didn't expect to see you in uniform, that's all. You should have told me you were on the team."

Charles shrugged. "Well, now you know."

Yes, she did. And she wasn't sure how she felt about that. They stood facing each other awkwardly for a moment. "Well. Good luck tonight," Ember said finally.

"Thanks. You too." Charles pointed toward her camera. "Make sure you get my good side."

Ember laughed and watched his retreating figure, allowing herself to wonder for just a moment whether that might count as his good side.

\*\*\*

Turned out, football was a lot harder to shoot than baseball. Ember could never be sure which way everyone was going to run, and most of the time the guy with the ball was covered up by a bunch of other guys. What if she shot the entire game and came away with nothing? By halftime she'd started to panic.

"Ember! You're here!" Claire ran up to her and gave her a hug.

It was an awkward sort of hug, because of the camera, but Ember couldn't help but smile. Somewhere in the back of her mind, she hoped her mom was watching. *Look, Ma, I'm making friends!* Girl *friends!* "I'm on assignment," she said, pointing to the camera and the press pass around her neck.

"On assignment? Like, for the *Bulletin*?"

"Yeah. I'm their newest photographer."

"Ahhh." Claire gave her a funny look.

"What's wrong?"

"Nothing. It's just … never mind. Congratulations. And good luck." Claire turned to walk away and then pivoted back around. "By the way, there's a party afterward. Want to come?"

Ember paused. Back home, parties meant drama and trauma. But it felt good to be invited, and maybe things would be different here. "I'll think about it. Catch up with me after the game."

Shooting the second half was easier. Ember started to get the hang of the action and the adjustments she needed to make for the crappy stadium lighting. Toward the end of the fourth quarter, the Bruins took the ball down the field to the six-yard line. A touchdown would almost guarantee a win. Ember crouched at the edge of the end zone and prepared to capture the big moment. She'd noticed that the team ran most of its plays toward the left side of the field, so that was where she stationed herself. *Please, please, let them come this way.*

Behind her, the crowd chanted, "Bru-ins! Bru-ins! Bru-ins!" Across the field, the school mascot, a kid wearing a huge, roaring bear head, was jumping up and down like crazy. If she was lucky, maybe she could catch him mid-jump in the background.

As the teams lined up for the play, Ember glanced toward the bench. Charles stood there, holding his helmet against his right hip and shouting to his teammates. Just a few feet beyond him, Claire waved her pompoms and performed impossibly high kicks. The crowd's roar intensified.

Ember shook her head. All this over a stupid game.

The play unfolded in slow motion. The quarterback dropped back and turned toward his left, just as she'd predicted. He passed to a receiver running straight toward her. Sweet.

Click. Click. Click. His form grew larger and larger with each shot. It was perfect. Until it wasn't. He scored, but he didn't stop. The play morphed from slow motion to warp speed as he barreled on. *What the* … Ember scrambled to get out of his way, but her feet tangled beneath her. She tripped. Landed hard. Her camera. She covered it with both hands. *Please don't break the camera.*

# CHAPTER SIX

**"S**he's coming to." The man's voice sounded far away. "Give her some space, boys. Back up!"

What had happened? The last thing Ember remembered, she was shooting Claire's backflip dismount from the pyramid at halftime, and now here she was lying flat on her back, head pounding. She reached up to rub her forehead, and her hand came away with blood on it. "Holy …" She tried to sit up, but the man stopped her. He had a shaved head and kind eyes. She recognized him as the head coach.

"You took a spill. You'll be all right." He held up his hand. "How many fingers?"

Ember squinted. Took a spill? How? In front of the

whole freaking stadium? She closed her eyes, trying to remember.

"Stay with me." The coach tapped her cheek. "I don't want you to fall asleep, understand? How many fingers?"

"Two."

"Good. What's your name?"

"Emily Slov—"

"Ember! Ember O'Malley!" Her mother's panicked voice cut her off.

"Mom?" Ember lifted her head to find her mother pushing through the crowd of players.

"Her name is Ember O'Malley."

The coach gave her mom a tense smile. "Thank you, ma'am, but I'm asking her. I want to make sure she's okay."

Her mom knelt down beside her. "Oh, *Ember*, you poor thing." Taking a packet of tissues from her purse, she began dabbing at the blood on her forehead.

Right. She was Ember now. And she was from Philadelphia. And … that was all she could remember. She tried to picture her cheat sheet, but it was a blur.

"What high school do you go to?" The coach continued his interrogation.

"What kind of a question is that?" her mom asked. "She goes here. To Boyd County High."

He sighed. "Ma'am, I know you're upset. But in fifteen years of coaching football, I've dealt with a lot of knockouts. Please. Allow her to answer for herself."

Her mom shook her head. "Enough questions. She needs medical attention. I'm taking her to the emergency room to have her checked out." She tried to help Ember sit up.

The coach grabbed her arm. "Ma'am, I would prefer to let her lie still for a few more minutes. She took a pretty serious blow."

"Fine. But no more questions."

"But, ma'am, she—"

Ember's mom leaned toward him and lowered her voice. "You may have coached football for fifteen years, but I've been her mom for sixteen. I win."

Ember wiggled her fingers and toes and tested her jaw. Every part of her ached, but it all seemed to be working. She touched her forehead again. More blood. "How bad is it?"

"Just a scrape." The worry in her mom's eyes told her otherwise.

"What happened? How did I—"

"Shh. Relax. Not another word until we get into the car."

Ember nodded. Her mom was right. They couldn't afford to take chances. One slip from her foggy brain and everything they'd done this week could be for nothing. They'd have to do it all over again, in another part of Nowheresville. This was all her fault to begin with. She couldn't put her mom and Tricia through it again.

What about that night? Did she remember it? Much as she hated to go there, she needed to be able to recall exactly what happened. Without her testimony, the truth would never come out.

Ember closed her eyes and allowed herself to go back, to feel the warmth of the bonfire and the tequila and hear the strum of the guitar as some guy in dreadlocks sang "One Love." To remember the panic she felt when she heard the shouts and the word "ambulance," and the helplessness that overcame her when she reached the water's edge and watched as Zach and Jimmy tried in vain to jump-start the girl's heart and force air into her lungs. There'd been no sudden gasp, no spurt of water, no convulsing, or coughing, or any sign of life at all. Just a limp body with stony eyes and lips the color of denim. Ember had raced back to the bonfire. She'd picked up the girl's beer and—

"Come on, Ember." The coach tapped her cheek. "Stay with us, sweetheart."

Ember's stomach churned as she opened her eyes and looked around. *Oh, God, please don't let me puke. Not here. Not with all these people staring.* She unzipped her coat. She was so hot. Was it the memory of the bonfire? The stadium lights? The fact that she'd almost blown her cover? Or maybe it was the fact that eighty-some boys in full football gear circled her, a pack of wolves eyeing a rabbit caught in the brambles. "I don't feel so good. Can we please leave?"

The coach nodded. He stood and signaled someone across the field, and within seconds, a beat-up mini golf cart trundled up beside them. Ember's stomach lurched as she stood, but she didn't throw up. As her mom and the coach helped her climb into the cart, Ember spotted Charles talking to her sister in the end zone. He was handing her something. The camera.

She grasped the empty spot in front of her chest where the camera should have been. She'd forgotten all about it. How could she? And how had Charles ended up with it?

# CHAPTER SEVEN

Deputy Steuben met them with a wheelchair in the emergency room lobby. Ember sank into it without protest. She didn't trust herself, or her stomach, to walk very far.

Deputy Steuben worked for the U.S. Marshal Service and was basically assigned to babysit her. He was short and stocky, and Ember guessed he was probably in his late twenties. He wore plain clothes— jeans, work boots, and a University of Iowa baseball cap. "Dr. Martinez will be the attending physician," he told her mom. "I've briefed him on … " He paused and glanced around. "Her situation."

The nurse eyed Ember curiously as she wheeled

her down the hallway. It probably wasn't every day a U.S. Marshal demanded to speak to the doctors about a patient. Had she guessed this was a Witness Protection case? Surely she couldn't think Ember was a criminal. Though her forehead had stopped bleeding, Ember held a cloth against it to cover her face.

Dr. Martinez treated her cut with something that stung like crazy and asked a bunch of questions. She was able to remember everything about her real past except for her old cell phone number, which wasn't that weird because she never called herself anyway. Her made-up past, though, was a different story. Ember O'Malley from Philadelphia. That was all she had. Not the name of her supposed high school, not her fake former address, not her mom's made-up old job, none of it.

Her mother pleaded with the doctor. "She has to be able to remember. It's important."

"We're going to run an MRI on her. If there's no severe trauma—which I don't think there is—it should come back to her, though it may take a day or two. If not, she'll have to relearn it." He dabbed Ember's forehead with more of the stinging stuff. "We should probably give her a couple of stitches on this cut, too."

Great. So now she'd be the new girl at school who'd made a spectacle of herself at the big game, couldn't remember even the simplest facts about her past, *and* looked like Frankenstein. So much for keeping a low profile.

Tricia had stayed in the lobby with Deputy Steuben, but the nurse brought her in to sit with them while they waited for the MRI results.

Ember held out her hand. "The camera. Hand it over." Was it damaged? She looked through the viewfinder at her mom and snapped a photo. It worked. Ember let out a long breath. She cringed as she scrolled through the shots from the game. Too dark. Too blurry. Too many butts and not enough faces. The halftime shots of the cheer squad were better, and then came the second half shots. She didn't remember taking any of them, but they were better, much better.

Finally, she reached the photos of the receiver charging toward her. They were brilliant. In the last one, she could see the whites of his eyes through his helmet slats. That explained a lot. The guy had to be six feet tall and a hundred seventy pounds of muscle. "Holy crap. *That's* what caused my 'spill'?"

Her sister laughed. "It was awesome. I mean, except for the part about you getting hurt, of course. But I wish I had a video of it."

Ember glared. "So then what happened?"

"Everyone sort of stopped and held their breath,"

Tricia said. "Except for Charles. He was the first one to reach you. He's super fast."

"Really?" Maybe Charles *was* a football superhero.

"Yep. Coach followed right behind him. He yelled at Charles not to move you, so he backed off. He did get the camera, though."

Of course. The camera. Charles was worried about saving the photos for next week's paper, not about her health and well-being. Maybe that could be a sidebar to the game coverage: *Football Superhero Makes Daring Camera Rescue.*

The nurse poked her head in. "Excuse me, Ember? You have a visitor."

A visitor? Ember, Tricia, and her mom all looked at each other. Who could it be? Ember's mind flashed to all the movies and TV shows she'd seen where the bad guys tracked down their victims as they lay helpless in the hospital. Was Deputy Steuben still around? Maybe he was lying out in the parking lot, his neck slit.

"Hey, girl!" Claire bounced into the room holding a teddy bear and a "Get Well Soon" balloon. "How do you feel?"

Ember breathed a sigh of relief, and her mom and sister exchanged nervous giggles. "Um. I'm okay, thanks. What … what are you doing here? Wasn't there a party?"

"Yeah. I went for a little while, but I left early so I could come by and see you."

"Oh. Well, thanks. You didn't have to do that."

"Psshh. It was boring anyway." Claire turned toward Ember's mom and sister. "Aren't you going to introduce me?"

"I'm sorry," Ember said. "I didn't mean to be rude. It's just … never mind." It was just that she wasn't used to having friends. People who cared about how she was doing.

"Nice meeting you," her mother said. "Very sweet of you to come by, but I'm afraid Ember needs to get some rest."

Ember rolled her eyes. Normally her mom would have fawned all over Claire and insisted she stay as long as she wanted. The only reason she was trying to get rid of her was because she was afraid Ember might screw things up.

"Oh, of course." Claire headed toward the door but then turned back around. "I know cell service in here is terrible. Do you want me to text or email anyone back in Philly to let them know what's going on?"

Her mom's face registered alarm. Ember widened her eyes in a silent plea for her to chill out. What did she think she was going to do, spill everything? "No, thanks." Ember said. "That's really nice, but … my mom can go outside and make some calls once we get the test results."

The doctor swept into the room, clipboard in hand. "Speaking of test results … " He paused and gave Claire a pointed stare.

"Guess that's my second cue to leave," she said. "Good luck, and call or text if you need anything. My cell number's on the back of the card." She pointed to a small get-well note tucked into the teddy bear's paws.

"Thanks." Ember smiled. Her first cell number here.

The tests all came back fine, so the doctor released Ember with a prescription for some mild painkillers and lots of rest. Deputy Steuben warned she should stay home from school Monday if her memory hadn't returned to normal. "And no more visitors," he advised.

\*\*\*

Being stuck in bed gave Ember plenty of time for her online stalking routine. All week, Zach had been posting about how much he missed her, how he hoped she was safe, how he wanted to see her again.

Saturday morning, though, was different. He posted

two photos from the night before: one of him toasting the camera with a shot glass and one of him sitting on some couch Ember didn't recognize with a way-too-cute girl leaning over his shoulder and smiling.

They didn't look like they were together. At least, not like that. Did they?

Ember stared at the shot for a long time. Zach couldn't be moving on already, could he? It had only been a week. Of course, he had no idea where she was or whether she was ever coming back. Everything had happened so quickly the day she left. She hadn't even had time to say goodbye. Her eyes filled with tears. She missed his easy laugh and the way his thick curls covered his eyes when they got too long. She missed the way he would trace his finger along the edge of her ear cuff, gently tickling her until she'd squeal and make him stop. If he had been there last night, he would have held her and kissed her just above her injured forehead and whispered to her that everything would be fine. And she would have let herself believe him.

For the millionth time in a week, she thought about doing what Deputy Steuben and her mom had said she must never do. What could it hurt? One quick message to tell him how much she missed him. A "like" on his page so he'd know she was out here somewhere, thinking about him.

But Deputy Steuben had insisted. There could be no contact with anyone back home. None. Zero. Zip. "Even the slightest slip could compromise the entire program and put you all in danger," he'd said.

But what if she contacted him through a fake account? If she was careful, if she kept her personal details out and remembered to log off every time, no one but Zach would ever need to know. She even had the perfect username picked out, something only he would recognize. She went onto Twitter and clicked "Create Account." Username: *@LilEmmieOakley*.

# CHAPTER EIGHT

*Seven months earlier*

The Shoot 'Em Up Studio's door alarm buzzed. *Bzz. BZZZZZ. Bzz.*

Emily sighed. Why would someone come in now, five minutes before closing time?

"Be with you in a minute," she called from behind the costume rack. She hung the baby-blue girl's pioneer hat on its peg and placed the Colt 45 in its holster. "Welcome to the wild, wild—" She swallowed her words at the sight of Jimmy d'Angelo and Brad Wahl leaning against the counter. "What do you want?"

"We want our picture taken." Jimmy eyed her from head to toe and back up again.

She tugged at her saloon-girl bustier. "Seriously.

Why are you here?"

"Seriously," Brad said. "He's going to be Butch Cassidy, and I'll be the Sundance Kid."

Emily eyed them. She and her mom had rented that movie a few months ago. Things didn't end too well for Butch and Sundance. A smile tugged at her lips. "No problem."

While Jimmy and Brad changed into their costumes, Emily arranged the set. She'd started working at Shoot 'Em Up the previous summer. At first, Mr. Ellerby had relegated her to cleaning the shop and ringing up the customers, but now he finally trusted her to stage and take the photos. Of course, they didn't get much business in February, even on a Saturday, but at her wages they only needed two or three sales a day to make a profit. Not that she cared. She loved Shoot 'Em Up and would have worked for free. Her favorite part was helping people pick out props and accessories to fit their characters. Whether it was a fluffy boa for a cute little girl or a fedora for a sweet old man, she had a talent for finding the perfect pieces.

"What do you think?" Jimmy emerged from the dressing room wearing jeans with chaps and nothing else. He puffed out his bare chest like one of her sister's kites.

Emily stifled a gag. "I think Paul Newman is rolling

over in his grave. Butch Cassidy wore a shirt, and no chaps." She pointed toward the derby sitting on top of the costume rack. "At least get the hat right."

Jimmy grabbed the hat and sauntered toward her, his gaze again wandering up and down. She turned and pretended to adjust the spacing of the bar stools on the set.

Jimmy's stupid video was pretty much ruining her sophomore year of high school. The now infamous "Slutkowski Striptease" had made the rounds until everyone at school saw it. Molly, her only "friend"—Emily couldn't help but think of the word in quotation marks now—stopped hanging out with her, and everywhere she went, girls whispered and guys stared. The handful of dates she'd had all ended the same way, with her allowing some slimy jellyfish of a guy to go too far and wondering how she could have been so stupid as to think this date might have been different.

Jimmy and his minions on the football team, meanwhile, made constant jokes about her, pressed up against her in the hallways, and generally acted like they owned her. She never said a word. In fact, she usually laughed and went along with it. What else could she do?

"You make a convincing whore." Jimmy grabbed her waist and pulled her toward him.

Emily slipped out of his grasp and swiveled one of the stools around, placing it between them. "I'm not a whore. I'm a bar maid."

Jimmy sneered and pushed away the stool. "I wasn't talking about the costume."

She took two steps backward and slammed into Brad. Where had he come from? "Come on, Slutkowski," he said. "With a costume like that, you know you want it."

Emily looked back and forth between them. She was used to their teasing, but this felt different. Her heart pounded, and she felt a drop of sweat trickling down beneath the laces of her bustier. They wouldn't pull anything here, would they? In the studio, in the middle of the boardwalk? She realized with a sinking feeling that the few shops that were open in February had probably just closed up for the night. She wished she hadn't covered the front windows with all those sample photos. Anything could happen in here, and no one would see. Part of her also wished the .38 Special in her garter wasn't a fake.

Brad gripped her arm, and Jimmy pushed her up against the bar. She knew she should scream, but she didn't.

She'd brought this on herself. Not just because of the video. Because of how she'd handled Jimmy and his friends and all those boys who'd treated her like their own personal plaything ever since. Would anyone believe she was the victim here? Or would they assume she'd led them on?

*Bzz. BZZZZZ. Bzz.*

The door. Emily had never been so happy to hear that sound. Jimmy and Brad backed away, and there in the doorway, silhouetted against the dark of night, stood Zach Reagan. Zach freaking Reagan. It was like something out of a Western, except instead of the hero wearing a holster and cowboy boots, he had on a surf parka and flip-flops.

"Hey. What's up?" he asked.

"Hey, Zach. These guys were … " Emily paused. Should she tell him? She wanted to. Zach was one of the few guys at school who didn't torment her, who actually called her "Emily." She could tell from the look in his eyes he suspected something was wrong.

"We were getting ready to have our picture taken." Jimmy spoke up. "I'm Butch Cassidy and he's … "

"Sundance." Brad gave Zach a salute.

Zach looked back at Emily. She could tell he didn't believe them. She should say something. This was her chance. Instead, she forced a smile. "Yeah. I was showing them how I wanted them to pose, here against the bar."

Zach's gaze moved from Emily to Brad to Jimmy and back again to Emily. "That's it?"

Emily shrugged, silently pleading for him to get it, to stand up for her, to play the Lone Ranger and stop the bad guys once and for all.

At last, Zach turned toward Jimmy, his eyes narrow slits. "Are you for real?" Emily could feel the tension crackling through the air.

Jimmy shrugged. "You heard her. She was showing us how to pose. That's all it was."

Zach shook his head and took a step toward him. "I don't mean that. I mean … " He pointed at Jimmy's chaps. "*That*. That has to be the worst Butch Cassidy costume I've ever seen." Zach laughed, and the tension dissolved, along with Emily's hopes for a rescue. Though really, who could she blame but herself? She'd had a perfect opportunity to expose her tormentors, and she'd blown it.

# CHAPTER NINE

"You're M.L. Martin?" Ember gaped at the back of Marissa's head. She never would have believed this girl was capable of taking such incredible photos. And if she had, she'd have bet good money Marissa would have used her full name on the credits. Of course, it did explain why she couldn't shoot the football games. Wouldn't want to interfere with her cheerleading ambitions.

Marissa shrugged and pointed at her monitor. "Which do you like better? The shot with Mr. Monroe's profile or the one where he's facing the camera?"

Ember searched for a flaw in either shot, but both were good. Really good. Damn it. Marissa, a.k.a. M.L., was probably incapable of taking a bad photo. "Where did you learn to take pictures like this?"

"My aunt's a photographer. She bought me my first camera when I was six." Marissa glanced up from her screen. "Stop picking at your face."

Ember dropped her hand to her side. Her stitches itched. They didn't look as bad as she'd feared, but between them and the bruise that had bloomed around her left eye, she felt hideous. Especially standing there next to Marissa. Her memory had returned halfway through the weekend. She'd thought about faking it for a few days so she wouldn't have to go to school looking like a roller derby queen, but she couldn't bear to worry her mom any more.

"There she is. Our newest linebacker." Charles appeared in the *Bulletin's* office doorway. His smile disappeared as he neared them. "Whoa. Does it hurt?"

Ember shook her head and turned away. She shouldn't have come. She'd wanted to go straight home after school, but Tricia was trying out for the middle school production of *Annie*, so her mom wouldn't be there for another hour. And she still wouldn't let them ride the bus—something about a movie she'd seen one time where a killer kidnapped a kid from a bus stop.

Charles circled around her and tilted her chin up so he could examine her face. "That was an intense hit.

You have officially been tackled harder and sustained more injuries than I have all year. In fact, all four years I've played."

How humiliating. Ember forced a smile. "Well, thank you for saving the camera. Very heroic."

"No problem." Charles either didn't catch the sarcasm in her voice or chose to ignore it. "You got some killer shots."

"Especially those last few." Marissa said it so sweetly, Ember couldn't tell if she was being sincere or making fun of her. Marissa pulled the photos of the receiver up onto the screen and pointed to the last shot. "I particularly love this one. Right before he mows you down."

"That's Deon Jackson," Charles said. "He felt horrible about hitting you."

"I know. He came up to me today during lunch and apologized. He must have said 'I'm sorry' a thousand times. Even gave me this." Emily pointed to a plastic daisy sticking out of her backpack.

"He gave you that? For real?" Charles looked surprised. And maybe a little jealous?

Ember plucked the daisy and stuck it into her hair. "Yes, for real. Very cute." She left it to him to wonder whether she was talking about Deon or the daisy.

Charles reached up. Ember thought for a moment

he was going to grab the flower, but instead he gently brushed the edge of her bruise. She winced but didn't pull back.

"I'm sorry, too," he said. "When I assigned you to the game, I had no idea—"

"Of course you didn't." Ember waved him away. "It's not that big a deal. The doctor said I'll heal up in a few days. Like it never happened."

A mixture of relief and admiration registered in Charles's eyes. "You're tough, you know that?"

Ember shrugged. Sometimes the line between weak and tough was as hazy as the horizon on a hot summer day. Did going topless in a video and messing around with half the football team make her weak or tough? How about moving fifteen hundred miles from home to escape her identity? How about the fact that she wanted to break into tears right now at the concern in Charles's eyes?

"Any assignments for me this week?" Marissa interrupted their moment. Ember had almost forgotten she was there.

Charles blinked and turned toward her, as though he'd forgotten as well. "Good question, and yes, I do have assignments. For both of you." He reached into his backpack and pulled out a tablet. "Ember, do you think you'd be okay to cover the game again? If not,

I'd understand." He looked at Marissa. "We all would."

"Oh, definitely," Marissa chimed in. "Not everyone is cut out for that type of thing."

Ember's eyes narrowed. Was she trying to imply the accident was somehow her fault or that she was a wimp? "No problem," she said. "I'd love to shoot the game."

"Great." Charles tapped the tablet. "The good news is this week's story will be about much more than just a football game."

Ember sat up. "More?" Like a real news story?

"Yes," Charles said. "This is homecoming weekend, so we'll need photos of the king and queen, the court, the floats … you get the idea."

Homecoming? Ember stifled a sigh. Not exactly what she'd had in mind.

"Your schedule will be a little different. The game is on Saturday instead of Friday night. There'll be a parade in the morning, the game in the afternoon, and the dance at night."

Homecoming dance? Ugh. Ember hadn't thought about how awkward dances might be at a new school.

Charles turned toward Marissa. "I need you to take some shots in the computer lab. I'm investigating a story on a possible breach of the school's online security codes." He waved his hand at both of them.

"Not a word about that to anyone."

Ember nodded and grinned. It would be a lot easier to get a cool shot of a float than of a bunch of computers.

Marissa glared, as though she knew what Ember was thinking. "Sounds serious," she said, her eyes fixed on Ember. "As in, front-page serious."

Ember met her gaze. So Marissa, a.k.a. M.L., wanted to compete? Fantastic. May the best shot win.

# CHAPTER TEN

For the fourth night in a row, Ember stared at her Twitter page, empty except for her avatar—a sepia-toned photo of Annie Oakley she'd copied off Wikipedia. She'd created the account, but she hadn't followed anyone, nor had she composed a single Tweet. She knew as soon as she followed Zach, as soon as he saw her username, he'd follow back. But then what? What would she say? Could she explain everything to him? And could she trust herself to stop at "I'm safe," without spilling her location?

She wished she could tell him everything. About her new hair color. About the silos and the manure smell, about Claire and Marissa, about the hit she took at the game, and about the stitches. But of course, she couldn't. She couldn't tell him any of that.

Ember went to Zach's profile page. She could at least let him know she was thinking about him. Zach was the only person on earth who knew her—really knew her—and loved her anyway. Here she was surrounded by people who didn't know the first thing about her, not even her real name. Even her mom and sister couldn't begin to understand all she'd been through for the past year. No one could but Zach.

As she hovered over his "follow" button, Ember noticed a new tweet, twelve minutes old.

> @surfgurrl FTW with 120 pts at Zippies.

Ember read it again. She squeezed her eyes shut. Zippies was their arcade. Actually, it was the only arcade on the boardwalk, but Ember thought of it as Zach's and hers. Zippies was where he'd taken her on their first pseudo-date. Zippies was where he'd won her a huge stuffed pink flamingo playing the ring toss and taught her how to get past Level Nineteen on Totem Destroyer.

So who was this surfgurrl? Ember's hand shook as she clicked on the name. She knew what she'd find, but somehow it still hurt, a punch to the gut. It was her. The girl from the photo. Pretty, blond, tan, and very surf-girl like.

Ember felt as though a huge wave was pushing her down, pressing her under, sending her flailing and tumbling out of control. She tried to take a deep breath but couldn't. It was as though her lungs, her chest, her heart were being crushed.

Zach had been her lifeboat for the past seven months. How could he abandon her so quickly? How could he meet some chick at a party and three days later take her to Zippies for … skee-ball, probably. One hundred twenty points had to be skee-ball. Ember had always sucked at it, but Zach loved to play. And of course surfgurrl would be a natural. Finally, he'd met someone who could surf and play skee-ball. She could probably catch a baseball, too. No doubt they had tons in common and looked adorable together and … had he kissed her yet?

Ember closed her eyes again and tried not to think about that. But now it was all she could think about. She lay down on her bed, and the stress of the past month—the night of the bonfire, the death threat, her fight with Zach, the deputies showing up in her living room, the move—it all came out in a torrent of tears. She cried until she had soaked her pillow, and then she lay still, with the exception of an occasional soft hiccup-sob, for what seemed like hours.

Finally, she got up and returned to her computer. She couldn't let the wave keep her down. She needed to recover her bearings and find the light. The surface was never more than a few feet away. Surely if Zach knew she was out here, thinking of him, he'd realize how much he missed her, how much he loved her. One Tweet and he'd leave surfgurrl behind like backwash on the shore. Ember had waited too long already. She needed to make the move, and make it now. She returned to Zach's page and clicked "follow."

***

"Stop. Please." Ember turned and glared at her sister sitting in the back seat of the car. "If you sing that song one more time, you can bet your bottom dollar I'll kick your you-know-what."

Tricia grinned and continued belting out the lyrics to "Tomorrow."

Ember reached back to pinch her leg, but Tricia fended her off. She'd gotten the part of one of the orphans in *Annie* and hadn't stopped smiling—or singing—since.

"You'll have to wear rags, you know. And smudgy

makeup. Not exactly glamorous."

Tricia merely increased her volume.

Ember gave up. She put in her earbuds, cranked up her iPod, and sang John Mayer as loudly as she could.

"All right, enough." Her mother reached over and pulled out one of the earbuds. "Both of you. No more singing."

Ember shot Tricia a gloating smile. Finally, some quiet. She checked her Twitter account on her phone for the millionth time that morning. It would be an hour later back in Jersey. Surely he'd seen her follow by now?

At last, her account showed she had one follower. She held her breath as she clicked it. It had to be Zach.

It was. Over the next ten minutes she refreshed a hundred times, but nothing else came up. No Tweets. No direct messages. Nothing but the follow.

She stared out at the fields passing by. Why didn't he DM her? Was he still angry? Maybe he wanted to apologize but didn't know how. Or maybe he was so wrapped up in surfgurrl that he didn't even care.

"Who are you texting over there?"

Her mom would kill her if she knew she was on Twitter, but Ember fought the urge to cover up her screen. No way she could see it from that angle. "Nobody. A girl from one of my classes."

"The one we met? Clara?"

Ember winced at the wisp of hope in her mom's voice. "It's Claire. And no. Just someone who had a question about an assignment. It's nothing."

They rode in silence until they arrived at the school. As Ember climbed out of the car, Tricia grinned at her and began singing again.

Ember slammed the door. Screw tomorrow. Zach had better contact her today.

# CHAPTER ELEVEN

*Two months earlier*

Emily pulled one foot up onto the board, then the other. She positioned them directly across the center, just as Zach had taught her. She tried to loosen her grip and stand, but she couldn't. Her fingers refused to let go.

*Whap!* The wave upended the board and her with it. The roar of the surf filled her ears and then disappeared as she plunged into a silent darkness. She tumbled for a moment, helpless and disoriented. The scrape of sand against her knees and the amused stare of a snot-nosed boy standing ankle-deep as she surfaced made her humiliation complete.

She turned to retrieve her board and caught sight of

Zach riding a wave, much bigger than the one that had humbled her. She marveled as he weaved up and down and around. So beautiful.

"You almost had that one," he shouted as they paddled back out together. "If you could get up a little more quickly … "

Emily forced a smile. Timing wasn't the problem. Fear was. She tried again and again, always with the same result. She'd manage to get her feet on the board and her butt in the air, but her fingers would cling to the edges like a starfish to the rocks. Wave after wave knocked her down and swept her onto shore, until at last Zach suggested they dry off and head to the boardwalk for some ice cream.

Emily ran for her towel before he could change his mind. She pulled a pair of jean shorts on over her swimsuit, slipped into her flip-flops, and twisted her hair into a knot at the top of her head. "Big Moo or the Dairy Dome?"

"Big Moo." Zach kissed her forehead. "Because I like watching you try to eat their super-sized waffle cones without getting ice cream on your nose."

Emily watched as he toweled himself off, first his hair and face, then his arms and chest, and finally his six-pack stomach. They'd been dating for five months, ever since that night he'd swept her away from Jimmy and Brad at the Shoot 'Em Up, but she still couldn't believe it, couldn't trust it. What did he see in her? He knew what everyone at school said. Didn't he care? He could have any girl he wanted, but when she'd pointed that out to him a few weeks ago, he'd shrugged and said, "I want you."

Why?

\*\*\*

Emily's phone buzzed as she took her first bite of mint chip ice cream. Her sister Trina, texting two simple words.

Trina: It's here.

Emily swallowed a squeal and replied.

Emily: Can you bring it to the Big Moo?

She savored the rest of her cone. Wait until Zach saw the photo. He'd be so impressed. She hadn't told him about the contest, because she'd been certain something would go wrong, that the judges would realize they'd made a terrible mistake and would take back the award. But now it was official. The magazine had finally arrived, with her shot on the cover.

"Why do you keep smiling?" Zach grabbed a napkin and wiped his chin. When she continued smiling, he wiped his nose and cheeks, then his chin again. "Seriously, what?"

"Can't a girl smile for no reason?"

"Maybe, but that smile says you're hiding something."

She laughed. He knew her so well. He knew her and liked her anyway. Why couldn't she accept that? "You'll find out soon enough. I have something to show you."

Zach leaned forward on his stool and kissed her. "Can't wait to see it." He kissed her again, his lips cool from the ice cream and tasting of black cherries. "Do you want another lesson tomorrow? You looked like you were having a good time out there."

Emily pulled back and studied his eyes. He was serious. Maybe he didn't know her so well after all. She shook her head. "Sorry. I have to work a double shift tomorrow."

Zach nodded and gave her a teasing smile. "Don't forget your piece."

Emily never dressed up at the Shoot 'Em Up any more. That was another thing Jimmy d'Angelo had ruined for her. But she still strapped the revolver to her leg with a garter. It was silly, really. Carrying a fake gun offered her about as much protection as carrying her camera—maybe less, because at least with her camera she could capture an image of her attacker as evidence—but she felt somehow safer with the cold, hard metal pressed up against her thigh. Zach called her Emmie Oakley, Little Sure Shot of the Jersey Shore. And she did have good aim. Beat him every time at the arcade shooting games.

"I could drop by to see you at lunchtime," he offered. "We could grab some pizza."

"Sounds perfect. I should be able to take a break at—" She stopped and grinned at the sight of her sister rushing through the door, waving a magazine in the air. "Wow, it really is here."

Trina stopped at their table and held the magazine up alongside her face. "I'm famous!"

Emily grabbed it, her hands shaking. The shot looked amazing. And there, in the lower right-hand corner, her name: "Teen Photo Contest Winner: Emily Slovkowski." She showed Zach. "I'm famous!"

Zach's eyes widened, and his mouth dropped open. "Whoa. When did this happen? Why didn't you tell me?"

Emily shrugged. "I guess I didn't believe it myself until now. I mean, it's kind of a big deal, right?"

"Yes, it's a big deal. It's a huge deal." Zach grabbed

the issue and turned to the people sitting at the next table, an older couple about her mom's age. "Check this out. My girlfriend took this. That's her sister, right there." He pointed to Emily and Trina.

"Stop. They don't care." Emily reached for the magazine, but the woman had already taken it.

"That's wonderful," she said. "Congratulations."

One of the Big Moo counter workers, who was wiping down a nearby table, came over to look. "Is that you?" he asked Trina. He turned to another customer. "Check this out."

Pretty soon half the restaurant had gathered around, admiring the photo and congratulating Emily.

"We should get some pictures of you two with the magazine," Zach said. "Give me your phones."

Emily and Trina posed together by the counter while Zach took photos. He kept saying, "smile," but he didn't have to. Emily couldn't stop smiling. She'd received lots of attention over the past year, but not like this. Her cheeks hurt from all the smiling.

Zach took several shots and then suddenly burst out laughing. Everyone who was watching started to laugh, too. For a moment, she thought they were laughing at her. Had they read her mind? Maybe it was silly to think she could ever amount to anything more than Emily Slutkowski. Then she turned around ... and came face-to-face with a gigantic cow head.

The Big Moo mascot was leaning across the counter between her and Trina.

"Best. Photobomb. Ever." Trina gave the cow a fist bump.

Emily turned back around and howled. So they weren't laughing at her. For once, she was part of the joke, not the object of it.

# CHAPTER TWELVE

Ember tucked the lens into a padded pocket, slung her camera case over her shoulder, and gave it a light pat. "Guess you're my date tonight." She could do worse.

Of course no one had asked her to the homecoming dance. She'd only been there two weeks. And anyway, she wouldn't have wanted to go. The only person she could imagine herself dating was half a continent away. Still, she couldn't help but wonder whether Charles was going, and if so, who his date would be. And how he'd look in a suit.

She checked her phone before heading out to the parade. This would be the last time she'd check it for the day. She was not going to obsess over Zach when she needed to concentrate on her photography.

She scrolled back through their Twitter messages—a total of thirty-eight DMs in the past three days, not that she was counting. At first, he was just super happy to hear from her and to know she was okay. He said he missed her and wanted her home. But then he started grumbling about how she should give up her "obsession" with testifying and come back to Jersey. Obsession? Because she wanted to do the right thing?

As she was reading, a new message popped up.

Zach: Weekends suck the most. Give it up and come home.

Damn it. She shoved her phone into her back pocket. She almost regretted contacting him in the first place. He didn't get it before she left, and he didn't get it now.

\*\*\*

Little kids and animals—every photographer's dream, and the parade had plenty of both. Especially animals. Horses, cows, goats, sheep. One kid even rode by with a chicken perched atop his bike's handlebars. Ember had never seen a parade like it. She wished she'd thought to bring along an extra card for her camera. She took nearly two hundred shots in the first hour.

At last, the marching band, the cheerleaders, and the final floats—the ones carrying the team and the homecoming court—came into view. Ember set her tripod at the edge of the route and adjusted her aperture settings to accommodate the bright noon sun. Charles had specifically directed her to get a good shot of the Homecoming Court, and she intended to blow him away.

The cheerleaders flounced by in a flurry of pompoms and backflips. Ember waved to Claire and noted that Marissa was nowhere to be seen. Of course. She must be part of the court. Pretty, talented, *and* popular. The high school trifecta.

The team floats rumbled by, sporting a mishmash of banners and flags and ribbons in the school colors, red and white. Some of the players rode in them, while others walked alongside them, handing out candy to the kids along the route. Directly across from her, a huge guy—he had to be a linebacker—crouched down to hand a lollipop to a little girl in a bright yellow-and-white polka dot dress. Her eyes grew big and round as she reached out to take it. So sweet. Ember snapped a photo, then another, then her viewfinder went black.

*What the* … She pulled away to find Charles standing in front of her, his hand over the lens. "Hey, there."

She narrowed her eyes, though she couldn't help but smile. "Don't you know better than to disturb the photographer when she's in her zone? You may have just ruined the best shot of the day."

Charles turned to follow her gaze. "That is a cute shot. But it's not the best shot of the day. That'll be tonight at the dance."

Tonight? He must mean the crowning of the king and queen. Did he really care about that stuff? Ember resisted the urge to roll her eyes. "Looking forward to it. In fact, here comes the float with the court. Don't want to miss that."

Charles nodded, handed her a piece of candy, and jogged away. "Back to your zone," he shouted over his shoulder. "See you this afternoon. Or tonight."

Tonight. So he was going to the dance. Ember's stomach performed a tiny flip, but she didn't have time to scold herself for it. The float carrying the court had stopped about twenty feet away.

Ember took a handful of wide shots, then zoomed in for some close-ups. Marissa looked amazing. She wore a simple purple and white strapless dress with a blue-green sash that should have clashed horribly but somehow didn't. She appeared perfectly comfortable in three-inch heels, even on a rickety float filled with bales of hay. She even managed to pull off the ridiculous tiara each of the girls was wearing. At one point, Marissa looked straight at Ember and smirked. Ember snapped the shutter, but too late. The smirk had morphed into an angelic smile.

As the float pulled away and the parade wound down, Ember packed up her camera. There, at the bottom of her case, sat the piece of candy Charles had given her. For the first time, she looked at it. A pink candy heart.

Her stomach did the flippy thing again. This time she did scold herself. Surely that was unintentional. He'd handed her a random piece of candy that happened to be the universal symbol of love. It meant nothing. And even if it was supposed to mean something, she wanted nothing to do with it.

She started to open the wrapper but then changed her mind and tucked it carefully back into her case.

# CHAPTER THIRTEEN

Ember grabbed the card and gave her mom a quick hug. "Thanks. You've saved my butt."

She turned and dashed back through the parking lot toward the stadium. Maybe she could still catch the end of the halftime show. "Never again," she muttered to herself. Forgetting her extra memory card was a total amateur move. She hoped no one noticed she hadn't taken a single photo for the final five minutes of the second quarter. Luckily, neither team had scored.

With a flash of her press pass, she slipped in through the entrance and cut to the left, toward the back of the bleachers. It was no shortcut, but it would allow her to avoid the meandering, snack-seeking halftime crowds.

Though it was mid-afternoon, the light was dim beneath the bleachers, and she had to watch her step to avoid the occasional puddle of soda or rotting hot dog that had fallen through from above. The marching band's hilarious mash-up of "Happy" and "Tears of a Clown" filtered in through the metal structure. How far along were they? Could she get into position in time to shoot their finale formation?

She had just stepped over what appeared to be a used condom—so gross—when she heard a noise. She stopped. She wasn't the only one under there. She squinted and made out two dark shadows up ahead. Please, not condom users. Anything but that. Her only choices were to turn around and go all the way back or to forge ahead, past the mystery couple. Only one of those choices would result in halftime photos.

She walked warily toward them and was relieved to realize it was two guys huddled together whispering. Then one handed the other a wad of money. A drug deal under the bleachers. How cliché. They probably wouldn't appreciate having company for it, especially not someone wearing a press badge and a camera. And really, the last thing she needed in Boyd County was to witness another freaking crime. Forget the halftime photos. She was going back.

She turned to leave when a shout stopped her.

"Who's that?"

Crap. They'd seen her. Nothing to do now but walk by. Perhaps if she pretended she hadn't seen a thing... "Oh, hey," she said, trying to keep her voice light. "Didn't expect to see anyone else under here."

She rushed past with what she hoped was a breezy wave. As she did, she recognized the guy who had handed over the money as one of the team's coaches. The other guy was a skinny kid with short, dark hair and a weak chin. Not that she cared. This was none of her business, and she had no intention of ever needing to identify either of them for any reason. Period.

\*\*\*

One peek. Just one. Ember checked her phone on her way into the dance. Nothing from Zach. Not that she could blame him. She hadn't responded to his last message, the one urging her to come home.

What was he doing right now? Was he with *her*? His homecoming was next weekend. What if he asked *her* to go with him? Ember had asked him about surfgurrl, of course. Turned out her name was Allie, and she was from the next town up the coast. Zach insisted they were just friends, but ... maybe he'd insisted too much.

Ember smoothed the light blue skirt of her dress. She wished Zach could see her in it. He'd run his hands along its fitted waist and tell her how beautiful she looked. He'd kiss her bare shoulder, on up to her neck and her earlobe, until she'd giggle and push him away. She sighed. Instead, she was here alone, standing outside the gym doors with no date and no real friends. It reminded her of last year, the pre-Zach era. Depressing.

"Your bruise is gone."

Deon Jackson was standing in the shadows of the hallway staring at her. She touched her eye. "Yeah. Like it never happened."

"I still feel bad about that. Glad you're okay."

Ember glanced around. Where was his date? For a moment, her heart lightened. Maybe he didn't have one. Maybe lots of people went to the homecoming dance without dates here.

"Thalia's in the bathroom," he said, almost as if he'd read her mind. "Girl takes forever in there."

She nodded and forced a smile. Of course he had a date. Everyone would, except her. She'd be the lone loser. As soon as she got those photos of the king and queen in their crowns, she was out of there.

Deon pointed to her camera case. "You taking the pictures?"

Ember nodded.

"Better get in there, then. Fun's about to start." Deon wore a devious smile.

Right. Time to take pictures of everyone else having fun.

The gym had been transformed into an undersea paradise. Glittery blue and silver streamers curved in long, elegant strips from the ceiling. Blue light coverings and a few carefully placed disco balls created the illusion of a watery shimmer. Seashells, conches, and starfish served as centerpieces on the scattered high-top tables.

As Ember took it all in, her eyes grew misty. She'd known coming to this would make her miss Zach, but she hadn't expected it to make her miss everything else about home too. The shore, the pier, the Shoot 'Em Up.

She clung to the shadows, taking occasional shots of the festivities, but for the most part trying to stay invisible until it was time for the court to be called on stage. During one of the slow songs, she saw Claire dancing with a boy she didn't recognize. He was tall, with blond hair like hers. Very cute. Ember managed to get a shot of the two of them without Claire seeing her.

After a few songs, she grabbed a glass of punch and a plate of mini tacos, found a table in the corner, and surveyed the scene. Where was Charles? She hadn't spotted him anywhere. Earlier she'd been anxious to see him and find out who his date would be. Now she hoped she'd get through the night without running into him. Better if he didn't witness her in all her dateless glory. Still, she couldn't help but wonder. Were he and his date running late? Or had they left early? Not that she cared. She popped a mini taco into her mouth. And another. She checked the time on her phone. *Let's get this show rolling.*

As she downed her last drop of punch, the music stopped. Toward the front of the room, someone shouted and a bunch of kids began hooting and whistling. Ember grabbed her camera. What was going on? A fight? Someone breaking out their dance moves? Or maybe it was finally time for the court to be crowned.

# CHAPTER FOURTEEN

Ember pushed through the growing crowd. The entire football team had formed four lines on the dance floor in front of the stage. One of them held up a fist and counted off: "One. Two. Three." The speakers crackled to life with "It's Raining Men," and everyone erupted into laughter as they broke into a pseudo flash mob routine with just the right mix of sexy and hilarious.

Ember stood, mouth agape, for a solid thirty seconds before she realized she should be taking photos. As she played with the focus, she spotted him. Second from the left in the back row, Charles stared straight at her. A playful grin tugged at the corners of his mouth, and she smiled back. He could dance. Really dance. The boy was full of surprises.

For the last verse, the guys ripped off their shirts and rushed into the crowd. Each of them grabbed the hand of the closest girl. A huge guy with a shaved head took Ember's hand and pulled her onto the floor. She tried to protest, holding up her camera, but he wouldn't take no for an answer. While all the girls stood laughing, the guys shimmied around them.

Ember danced and sang along as the players waved their hands in the air and shouted "Hallelujah," but just as the song ended, one of the guys bumped into her, pushing her into Shaved Head Dude's chest. He and another player grabbed her arms to steady her, but Ember suddenly felt smothered, boxed in.

A creep show flashed through her mind—Jimmy and Brad closing in on her at the Shoot 'Em Up, guys pawing at her in the backseats of cars, a tub full of football players ogling her as she dangled a bikini top in the air over and over and over. Her stomach lurched.

One of the guys stepped back. "You okay, Red?"

"Yeah, I'm … I need some air."

As she turned to leave, Charles appeared. "What did you think?"

She blanched, and without answering, ran through the crowd and out into the hallway. She made it to the girl's bathroom just in time. Those mini tacos were a horrible idea.

Afterward, as she splashed cold water on her face, Claire peeked in. "You all right? You acted like you saw a ghost."

Ember grabbed a paper towel and dabbed at her smeared mascara. "I think I had a bad taco. Stay away from those."

Claire walked over and gave her back a tentative rub. "I'm sorry. You looked awfully cute out there dancing, though. I love your dress."

Ember teared up again. Claire was so sweet. She wished she could tell her everything. About the GIF, about the horrible year she'd had, about Zach and how he'd made everything better. Maybe even about the murder. Claire might understand, might even forgive her for her part in all of it. But of course, she couldn't tell. Not Claire. Not anyone.

"That guy you were dancing with is really cute." Ember scrolled through the photos on her camera. "I got a great shot of the two of you."

Claire peered over her shoulder at the shots. "That's Ryan. Last year he was Lancelot and I was Guinevere. But we're just friends."

Something about the way she said it made Ember wonder if that was how Claire really felt. "Well, you look good together. Like a couple. Just sayin'."

Claire's blush told her all she needed to know.

By the time they returned to the gym, the homecoming court had already lined up across the stage. Thank goodness. Ember could take the shots and go home. The crowning ceremony was every bit as lame as she'd expected, though at least Marissa wasn't named queen. That was something.

As the court left the stage, she glimpsed Charles on the other side of the room. He was with a girl whose back was to her. She wore a simple black dress with pumps. She was tall, with long, dark curls that cascaded all the way down to her butt.

Of course. She would be beautiful, glamorous, and brilliant. Charles was no doubt madly in love with her.

Ember nudged Claire. "Who is that?"

Claire craned her neck. "That's Mrs. Bonner. From the chemistry department."

"A teacher?" Ember tried to say it casually, but Claire broke into a teasing grin.

"Yes. A teacher."

"So not a date?"

"Um. Pretty sure Charles wouldn't be dating a teacher. Or vice versa. As far as I can tell, he's here alone."

Ember turned away. If he didn't have a date, why

hadn't he asked her? She felt partly relieved and partly upset, and completely annoyed at herself for feeling anything at all. Charles was under no obligation to ask her. He was a friend. Maybe not even a friend, maybe just a boss. Besides, she loved Zach, and Zach loved her, and she wasn't going to let some meaningless homecoming-dance-insecurity thing trick her into thinking she cared about some guy who just happened to—

"Nice dress."

Ember turned to find Charles standing beside her. Claire had disappeared. "Oh." Her hands shook as she smoothed her skirt. "Thank you."

"Sorry about that dance." Charles motioned toward the spot where Ember had freaked out earlier. "With the stripping and all. A few of us guys came up with it, and we thought it would be funny, but I guess it was more like obnoxious."

"No, no." Ember shook her head. He must think her a total prude. "It was cute. Awesome. But I … "

She what? Had a flashback to her former life, where she was a complete loser slut who had no friends and no boundaries and certainly not the guts to change anything? She stared down at her shoes. "I didn't feel well, that was all. I needed to get some air."

Charles said nothing for a moment. Finally, he put

his hand on her lower back. "Do you feel better now?"

She met his gaze and smiled. "Much better."

Charles grinned. He pointed toward the dance floor. "Well enough for a dance?"

A slow Adele song had come on, and in an instant the floor had transformed from a typhoon of gyrating bodies to a tranquil sea of swaying couples.

Ember hesitated as Zach's smile, his voice, and his saltwater scent swam through her mind. She should say no. Zach wouldn't want her dancing with another guy. On the other hand, what could it hurt? How was this any worse than playing skee-ball at Zippies with a "friend"?

She held up her camera case. "Let me hide this." She tucked the case behind the stage and returned.

Charles took her hand and led her out onto the dance floor. "Is this like your homecoming dances back in Philly?" he asked.

"Pretty much. In fact, I'd say it's exactly the same, but with more country music. The parade, on the other hand … that was different. So many animals."

Charles grinned. "We like our animals."

"Do you have any? Animals, I mean."

He laughed. "About seven hundred."

"Seriously?"

"My dad raises cattle."

Ember tried to imagine what it would be like to live on a farm with seven hundred cows. "Do you have to help out? With feeding and herding and … branding and stuff?"

"I guess. But I'm no cowboy, if that's what you're getting at."

A cowboy. It hadn't even occurred to her. He seemed so … nerdy. For the first time, she noticed how rough his hands were, how defined his arms, how tanned his face and neck. She stifled a smile. He was a nerdy cowboy. A nerdy, strip-dancing, football-superhero cowboy. She closed her eyes and leaned in toward him, allowing his solid frame and Adele's voice to calm her. For the first time in what seemed like years, she felt safe, almost at home.

The feeling didn't last long. Partway through the song, she felt a vibration in her dress pocket. Her phone. Zach had finally messaged her again. She knew she should wait until the end of the dance to read it, but she couldn't. She needed to know what he was thinking.

Ember stepped back and offered Charles an apologetic smile. "Sorry. I should check this." She pretended not to notice the look in his eyes—was it hurt? disappointment?—as she retreated to a corner and woke up her screen.

```
Zach: Luv u.
```

Her hands shook, and she leaned against the gym wall. This was the first time he'd said he loved her since the night of the murder, since all the fighting began. She hadn't realized how much she'd needed him to say it.

She looked up at the scene around her, at all the fake beach stuff and the room full of strangers dancing. She didn't belong here. She belonged back in Jersey with Zach.

Ember walked around the outside of the room to the stage. It was time to retrieve her camera and leave. She picked up the case and opened it to make sure no one had touched anything. Everything was in its place. The camera, the lens, the flash. And as she zipped the case closed, she spotted a flash of pink at the bottom. The candy heart.

# CHAPTER FIFTEEN

Ember leaned over Charles's shoulder and pointed at the screen. "Who's that kid?"

He'd pulled up a series of photos of a Bruins lineman sacking the other team's quarterback. Behind the action, sitting in the bleachers, the skinny kid from the drug deal stared straight into the camera. His glare gave Ember the chills. Had he watched her like that the entire second half?

Charles shrugged. "Seen him around, but I don't know. He's a sophomore, maybe."

At least that meant Charles probably wasn't involved. Not that it mattered. He could be the biggest cokehead in the world and she wouldn't care. She loved

Zach. Zach loved her. No more thinking about Charles.

He zoomed in on the kid's face. "If looks could kill, you'd be slaughtered, butchered, and frozen about now." He turned in his seat to face her. "Was this dude bothering you?"

"No, not at all." Ember tried to sound casual. "I've never seen him before either. I only noticed him because of his expression, but probably I just caught him as he was about to sneeze or something."

Charles scrolled through the series. "For six frames?"

"It's a fast shutter."

Charles shrugged and continued scrolling, apparently satisfied with her explanation. He stopped at a shot of a Bruins interception. "Nice. Maybe we'll use this one for the front page."

Ember's eye went immediately into the stands. There was the kid again, but he was watching the play. Thank goodness. "Enough game pictures," she said. "Let's check out the photos from the dance."

As Charles pulled them up, Marissa breezed in, flung her backpack onto the desk, and joined them at the monitor. "I get veto power over the homecoming court shots."

Charles grinned and assumed an official tone. "The editor in chief shall make the final determination on all

*Bruins Bulletin* content, including both editorial copy and images."

Marissa nudged him. "If the editor in chief wants his lead photographer to continue working for him, he'll give her veto power over the homecoming court shots."

Ember couldn't help but notice that she stressed the words "lead photographer." Of course she would want to throw that in her face. "Don't worry, Marissa. You look great in every shot." She did. Depressing, but true.

Marissa sat down at another computer and connected her camera. "I took some photos in the computer lab this morning. What's going on with that story?"

"Right now, there is no story." Charles lowered his voice, though the three of them were the only ones in the room. "The front office knows someone has hacked into the system, but they don't know who or why. And they can't ask too many questions, because they want whoever is doing it to keep doing it so they can catch them."

"So it's someone inside the school?" Ember asked. "Is it a student or a teacher?"

"They don't know for sure. They can't figure out why it's being hacked, but they know there's been a breach."

Marissa pulled up a shot of a darkened lab. Banks of computers and other electronics glowed throughout the room like a Christmas display gone awry. Off to one side of the shot, one lone monitor was lit up in the center, as though it had just been turned on. Clearly the shot was staged, but still. Amazing.

"What do you think?" Marissa wasn't asking Charles. She was asking her.

"I like it," Ember choked out. "Really good."

She didn't trust herself to say anything else. Marissa had done it. Her single shot of an empty computer lab was better than Ember's four gigs of homecoming parade, game, and dance photos. Marissa's shot intrigued the viewer, made them *feel* something. You could practically hear the soft, creepy horror movie music in the background.

For the first time in her life, Ember felt like a hack as a photographer.

"There it is!" Charles was still scrolling through her dance photos. "That's the money shot."

Ember turned to look. There on the screen, as big as life, a laughing Charles was ripping off his shirt. She'd zoomed in on him at just the right moment. That photo made her feel something, too, though she didn't want to admit it.

"Who's that kid who keeps showing up in your

photos?" Marissa appeared behind them.

"What kid?"

She pointed to the screen. There in the background, almost hidden in the shadows behind Charles, stood the skinny kid. Once again, he was looking into the camera.

"What do you mean, he keeps showing up?" Charles asked.

"Well, I've only seen a few dozen shots since I walked in, but that's, like, the third one he's been in, and he's always staring at the camera."

Charles started scrolling backward and stopped at the photo of Claire and Ryan on the dance floor. "You're right. There he is again."

Ember shuddered. This guy was starting to creep her out.

"Didn't you notice him?" Marissa asked.

Ember shook her head. "I guess not."

Marissa gave a dramatic sigh. "That's my photographer's eye. Always hyperaware of the background. I almost wish I could look at photos without it."

Ember took a deep breath. *We get it, Marissa. You're the real photographer here.*

"Maybe he has a crush on you," Marissa said with a smirk.

Charles stood and faced her, concern etched on his face. "Ember, what's going on with that guy? Seriously, if he's stalking you or something … "

Ember looked back and forth between him and Marissa. Should she tell them about her run in under the bleachers? After all, the man buying the drugs was one of Charles's coaches. Maybe he had a right to know what was going on. Then again, the last thing she needed was to be a witness to another crime scene. Why did drama follow her wherever she went?

"Don't be silly," she said. "I'm sure it's nothing. Maybe Marissa is right. Maybe he has a crush." She assumed her best sultry-movie-star voice and brushed her hand suggestively through her hair. "I've been known to have that effect on men."

Was it her imagination, or did Charles blush?

Ember grabbed the mouse, scrolling back to the shot of shirtless Charles. "I vote you run this one on the cover. Above the fold."

Marissa laughed. "I second."

Charles laughed. "As I said, the editor in chief makes the final determination. Not happening."

"Speaking of … " Marissa sat down in Charles's seat. "Time to check out the homecoming court shots."

"I like the ones I took during the parade better than the ones from the dance," Ember said. "More colorful, and better lighting." She felt her stomach clench as Marissa reviewed them. They seemed so boring, so pedestrian compared to her work. Fortunately, Marissa seemed concerned only with her own facial expressions.

"Yes. Yes. Yes. No. Yes. Yes. No." She flipped through them, dragging the ones she approved of onto the desktop. Never mind if the other members of the court were blinking or frowning or, in one case, actually yawning. Ember rolled her eyes. Guess Marissa's "photographer's eye" couldn't see past her own face.

As she neared the end of the parade shots, Marissa stopped at a photo of Tricia. "Who's this?"

Ember grinned. Her sister looked so cute. She'd had the Bruins logo painted onto her cheek and was waving a small American flag. "That's my sister, Tricia."

"She's a cutie," Charles said.

"Have I met her before?" Marissa asked.

"I doubt it."

Marissa zoomed in closer on Tricia's face. "Are you sure?"

"Yeah. I mean, since we moved here, she's come to both of the games, so maybe you've seen her in the stands, but I don't think you would have met her."

Marissa shook her head. "Something about her seems really familiar. Like I used to know her. I think it's the eyes and the smile."

A small knot formed in Ember's stomach. The *PhotoPro* cover. Marissa probably subscribed. She probably had the July issue somewhere in her house right now, among a pile of photography magazines. And while Tricia looked very different today than she had on that spring morning, with Marissa's eye …

"Are you okay?" Charles was staring at her. "You seem a little pale."

"No, I'm fine." Ember forced a smile. She reached over Marissa's arm, grabbed the mouse, and clicked past the shot of her sister.

# CHAPTER SIXTEEN

*Five weeks earlier*

"**W**hy can't I go to the bonfire?"

Emily sighed. She hated when Trina whined. "Because I don't need you tagging along. Because you're in grade school. Because you'd have to be home by ten for your bedtime. Should I go on?"

Trina sat down on Emily's bed and pouted. "It's not fair. Eighth grade is practically high school. And anyway, Mom let me stay up until eleven the past two weekends."

Emily snapped on her mermaid ear cuff and swept her hair behind it. "Well, you're not coming, so get over it." She pointed to the eyelash curler lying beside Trina. "Hand me that."

Trina watched her every move as she put on her makeup. "Are you going to teach me how to do my eyes like that this year? With the dark corners?"

"Maybe."

"And my lips? With the liner?"

"Sure." She wished Trina would leave her alone. She wanted to get ready in peace. This would be the last beach party of the summer, and Emily wanted to savor every minute of it, even the getting-ready part. She wasn't sure what the new school year would bring. Would the fact that she had seriously dated Zach all summer make a difference? Would her *PhotoPro* cover shot earn her some respect? Or would she be doomed to another year of people whispering and laughing behind her back, with Jimmy d'Angelo and company still treating her like they owned her?

"Em?"

"Yeah?"

"Do you and Zach kiss ... and stuff?"

Emily smeared her eyeliner. Damn it. This was not a talk she wanted to have. Not tonight. Maybe not ever. It wasn't so much what she and Zach had done that worried her. They really hadn't done much more than kiss. But she didn't want Trina to know what she'd done with all those other guys. She dabbed at the smear below her eye with a cotton ball. Next year, Emily would be a senior and Trina would be a freshman, and there would be no more hiding her reputation from her kid sister. But she planned to keep up the charade for one final year, to be the big sister Trina looked up to for as long as she could fake it.

"Yes. We kiss. Not that it's any of your business."

"How do you get a guy to want to kiss you?"

Emily whirled around and pointed her eyeliner pencil in Trina's face. "Oh, no. Ain't happening. You are too young to kiss boys, got it?"

Trina rolled her eyes. "I'm practically in high school."

"Yeah, well. Don't be in such a hurry to get there. It's not all rainbows and butterflies."

Trina stuck out her tongue and stalked out of the room. Emily grinned. At least she was still kid enough to stick out her tongue.

\*\*\*

Zach waved to her from across the beach, his tanned, muscled abs and biceps reflecting the amber glow of the bonfire.

Emily slipped out of her flip-flops and quickened

her pace. The cool sand shifted slightly beneath her feet as she neared the crowd, and the soft lilt of a guitar blended with the roar of the surf. Out of nowhere, tears sprang to her eyes, and the flames blurred into a hazy, glowing pyramid. Why did summer have to end?

"What's wrong, babe?" Zach wrapped his arm around her waist and kissed the top of her head.

She sank into him and wiped her eyes. "Nothing. It's just the heat from the fire."

He lifted her chin and kissed her, a warm, soft, lingering kiss. If only she could stand here like this with him forever.

"I was just getting ready to play some volleyball. You in?"

Ember eyed the court. Jimmy and Brad were high-fiving an ace serve. She wrinkled her nose and shook her head. "You go ahead. I want to chill for a while."

She poured herself a tequila sunrise from a nearby cooler, found a piece of driftwood near the guitar player, and sat down. He had long dreads with beads woven through, and he played a magical mixture of reggae and calypso. A light breeze blew off the ocean, while a full moon painted a soft gold streak through the water. If this wasn't heaven, she didn't know what was.

"Mind if I sit here?" A girl Emily had never seen before pointed to the edge of the driftwood.

"Sure."

The girl was pretty, with long, wavy dark hair and brown eyes that danced in the light of the fire. "I'm Rosa. Where are you from?"

"Hi, I'm Emily." She motioned toward the boardwalk. "I'm from here."

"Wow." Rosa looked out toward the water. "Lucky you."

"Yeah."

Rosa motioned toward the volleyball game. "He's cute."

Emily followed her gaze. She was watching Jimmy. Ugh.

"Good kisser too."

She'd kissed him? Maybe Emily should warn her about what a jerk he was. Then again, she was a tourist. She'd be gone in a few days. What could it hurt for her to have a late-summer fling with him? Emily pasted on a smile and turned away. She didn't want to talk, certainly not about Jimmy d'Angelo. She wanted to lose herself in the music, the breeze, the moonlight.

Rosa seemed to get it. She sat and sipped her drink, swaying to the music. Neither of them spoke another word.

Emily pulled her knees in tight and closed her eyes. The night couldn't be more perfect.

# CHAPTER SEVENTEEN

Deputy Steuben eased himself onto the couch. Ember knew why he'd come, though she pretended not to. "Didn't expect to see you this evening. What a surprise." She hoped she wasn't laying it on too thick.

"Can I get you a cup of coffee?" her mom asked.

He nodded. "Cream. No sugar. Thank you."

Ember sat down across from him. It was almost ten o'clock. She'd begun to think he might not show up. Thank goodness he had. She had so many questions.

As soon as her mom reappeared with the coffee, Deputy Steuben got down to business. "There's been a small setback."

Ember knew what was coming. Zach had messaged her about it last night. Apparently the news was spreading quickly back home. Of course, she couldn't tell the deputy or her mom about that.

"The toxicology reports came back inconclusive."

"What?" Ember feigned surprise. "But you said the tests would provide the key evidence, that my testimony was just to back them up." She'd tossed and turned all night after getting Zach's message. How could the tests be "inconclusive," and what did that mean for the case? Would the prosecutor drop it without them? Was it possible Rosa hadn't been drugged after all? What if Ember was wrong about everything? Maybe Zach was right. Maybe this was all for nothing. Maybe she should drop it and go back home.

Steuben leaned forward, placed his elbows on his knees and rubbed his eyes. He glanced back and forth between her and her mother. "We suspect intimidation."

"Intimidation? Of the coroner's office?" Ember's mom's hands shook, sending her coffee cup rattling across its saucer. She set it down and began to pace. "Good Lord. What are these people capable of?"

Ember's stomach twisted into a knot. Intimidation. Of course. Just as they'd tried to intimidate her.

"Either the coroner's office or the lab itself. Either way, they wouldn't go to these lengths if this thing didn't run deep. The kid was a minor. They'd let him take the rap. Most likely he'd get involuntary and be out in six to eight. No, they're not worried about that. They're protecting the business."

Ember nodded but said nothing. She didn't care about "the business," though sometimes she thought that was all Deputy Steuben did care about. He and the feds wanted to bring down some huge drug operation and maybe even a few high-level Mafia guys. Whatever. Ember just wanted to bring down "the kid," to prove to everyone what a scumbag he was and to keep him from hurting anyone else.

"So what now?" she asked. "Is it over? Do I go home?"

"No. This makes things tougher, but we still have a case." He paused and gave Ember a pointed stare. "If anything, it means your testimony is more important than ever."

Her mom crouched down beside her and placed her hands on her arm. "You don't have to do this, sweetheart. You can back out anytime. Like I've said all along, I'll stand behind you either way. So will Tricia."

Tricia. She'd gone to bed an hour ago, exhausted from her busy day of school, rehearsal, and homework. She was a big part of the reason Ember was doing this. Ember wanted—*needed*—to teach the Jimmy d'Angelos of the world that they couldn't treat girls like ragdolls and get away with it.

Ember looked Deputy Steuben in the eye. "I'm still in. Whatever you need."

He smiled and stood. "Good girl. We expect to know the trial date soon. It'll be sometime in early December. As soon as we know an exact date, I'll call you."

Early December. Two months away. She knew she should be worried about a thousand other things, but she had just one thought: Would she get to see Zach while she was there?

\*\*\*

The stadium was so quiet and unassuming when it was empty. Ember sat partway up the bleachers at midfield to watch football practice. She had the best seat in the house, but so far she was bored out of her mind. "Practice" seemed to consist of a bunch of endless stretching. Were they ever going to run drills or maybe line up to scrimmage?

Charles had assigned her to a photo shoot of

Coach Sebastian. He was the team's defensive coach. He was also the one she'd seen under the bleachers at homecoming. Ember would rather shoot just about anything else—an empty field, a montage of "the many faces of Marissa," or maybe selfies of her own root canal—but apparently the Bruins defense was breaking all kinds of records this year and Charles planned to run a big story featuring their rising-star coach.

Ember glanced through her notes. She'd planned to take some action shots during today's practice, some of the coach posing with the defensive players lined up behind him, and some of him in the athletic office, next to the trophy case. It seemed like a great mix, though she was starting to worry whether the "action shots" would consist of him sitting on the bench examining his clipboard.

Finally, almost twenty-five minutes into practice, the players began milling around and forming groups. The defense lined up on the side of the field closest to Ember to tackle a pair of stand-up dummies. As Ember grabbed her camera and moved closer, she peered across the field at the special teams players. There was Charles, kicking an imaginary ball over and over and over. Four steps ... kick ... and hold for the follow through. His movements were so precise, so smooth, it reminded her of Zach's pitching windup and release.

She took a deep breath. Two months. She could do this.

"Can I help you?" Coach Sebastian appeared at her side.

Ember pasted on what she hoped was a reassuring smile, one that said: *I come in peace. I have no interest whatsoever in your sub-bleacher activities.* "I'm with the *Bruins Bulletin* and I'm here to take pictures. Of you."

The coach grinned. "Is this for the article Charles mentioned?"

Ember nodded and pointed to her notes. "I thought I'd start with a few candids of you working with the team."

"Sounds good." If he recognized her, he didn't let on. It had been pretty dark under there. Maybe he hadn't gotten a good look at her.

Ember took dozens of shots of the practice. Coach Sebastian wasn't afraid to mix it up with his players, and they clearly idolized him. It was hard to believe this guy could be involved in anything illegal. He had such an easy laugh and seemed so ... likeable. Maybe she was wrong about him. Then again, people didn't hand over large wads of cash in dark, secluded places for Girl Scout cookies. Just like beer didn't turn blue all by itself.

After practice and the staged team photos, Ember

followed Coach Sebastian inside for the trophy room shots. "Charles says our defense is really good this year," she said.

Coach nodded. "This is my fourth year, and this is by far the best crop of kids I've had. Our front line is unstoppable." He went on to share the details of each position and how it was performing, most of which meant nothing to Ember. As they entered the trophy room, he paused, a frown spreading across his face. "Wait a minute. I know who you are."

Ember tensed. He'd finally recognized her. "Listen, Coach. About that. Let's not go there. I was in the wrong place at the wrong time. As far as I'm concerned, nothing happened. Okay?"

The coach shrugged. "Sure. If that's what you want. But watch yourself from now on, you hear?"

A shiver ran up her spine. Was he threatening her? "What do you mean, watch myself?"

His eyes narrowed. "Listen, I'm a competitive guy, so I get it. I understand you wanted to capture the perfect shot, but it's not worth getting killed. You get that close to the edge of the end zone, you're practically asking to be run over."

Ember smiled, relief spreading through her. "Oh, that!"

"Yes, that. What did you think I was talking about?"

"Nothing. I mean, I knew you were talking about that. And you're right. It was foolish of me. Like I said, wrong place at the wrong time. I've learned my lesson." She pointed to the trophy case. "Now, how about we finish up this shoot so we can both go home?"

The rest of the shoot went smoothly. Ember felt as though a huge weight had been lifted off her. Coach Sebastian didn't recognize her from their meeting under the bleachers. Maybe she really could put the whole incident behind her.

Ember took a shortcut through the athletic office on her way out of the building. As she passed the football coaches' cubicles, a movement caught her eye. Someone was back there. A shiver prickled at the back of her neck as she paused and listened. She shook her head. She was being silly. It was no doubt one of the other coaches working late, or maybe a janitor. She picked up her pace, but as she turned the corner, someone stepped out in front of her.

It was the drug-dealing kid, wearing the same creepy stare he'd worn in the photos.

"Hello, Emily."

# CHAPTER EIGHTEEN

It took Ember a moment to realize what he'd said. *Emily.* Her pulse quickened. Who was this guy? How did he know her? "Excuse me? It's Ember," she said, her voice an unconvincing squeak.

The kid sneered. "No, it's not. I know exactly who you are. And I think I know why you're here."

Ember's legs began to shake. Could this guy be connected to Jimmy's crowd? She considered his long, scraggly hair and his skeletal frame. He wore thin-rimmed glasses and a T-shirt promoting some video game she'd never heard of. Not exactly the typical Mafia hit man, but then how did he know so much?

"Don't worry," the kid said. "I'm good at keeping

secrets. That is, so long as you keep your mouth shut. What you saw last week stays between you, me, and Coach."

Ember fingered her camera strap, struggling to keep her expression calm as her mind raced. Another threat. Exactly what she'd come here to escape. She'd have to tell Deputy Steuben about this. No. No, she couldn't. She should, but that would ruin everything. They'd have to pick up and move again, and find a new home, and settle in at a new school, and … and Charles wouldn't be at the new school. Which was totally immaterial. Crap.

"Who the hell are you?" she asked. "And what makes you think you know so much about me?"

"I go by Tommy. Which, by the way, is my actual name. Strange as that may seem."

Ember's eyes narrowed. "Well, Tommy, I may go by a different name, but at least I don't make a habit of skulking around beneath the bleachers at halftime."

"Like I said, you keep my secret, I'll keep yours."

Ember said nothing. That was fine with her. She had no intention of ratting him out anyway.

He held out his hand. "Deal?"

Ember didn't trust him or his slimy handshake, but what choice did she have? She only hoped he was so scared of getting caught that he'd keep his mouth shut. She shook his hand. "Deal. But you so much as look at me funny in the hallways, and I'll go straight to the authorities." She stepped around him and stalked away. "And if you know so much," she shouted back over her shoulder, "you know I have easy access to certain authorities."

\*\*\*

Claire held up a gray-and-white striped sweater. "What about this?"

Ember shook her head. "No stripes or patterns. Too distracting."

She was spending the night at Claire's, and they'd decided to do a photo shoot for her acting portfolio. Ember could hardly remember the last time she'd slept at a friend's house. Actually, she did remember, though she wished she could forget. It was that night at Molly's.

"This one?" Claire slipped on a light blue tunic and turned toward the mirror.

"Perfect. Brings out the blue in your eyes."

"So, here's my idea." Claire jumped on the bed beside her. "I, of course, need a large portrait—that's what everyone does. But I was thinking, what if I had a strip across the top with a bunch of smaller shots too?"

"Thumbnails."

"Exactly. With lots of different poses and expressions, to show my range."

Ember nodded. She knew nothing about acting portfolios, but it seemed like it could work. "Sure. That'll be fun."

The shoot took almost two hours. It probably could have been over in half the time if it weren't for Claire's hilarious fake poses. Ember's cheeks and sides hurt from laughing by the time they'd finished. "You realize I have some great blackmail material here?" she said as they scrolled through the shots. "Here's my favorite: Claire Lockman, crazed circus clown."

Claire howled. "Circus clown? That was my Lady Macbeth impression." She tapped the screen. "We should get that up on Facebook."

"Are you serious?" The shot was hideous. If anyone ever took a photo like that of her, Ember would make them delete it immediately. But Claire never seemed to care what people thought. She did whatever she wanted, said whatever she wanted, and hung out with whomever she wanted.

"Of course I'm serious. We can ask for captions. Why don't you load it up to your page and share it?"

Uh oh. Ember blanched. She did have an Ember O'Malley page, but it was practically empty. She'd maxed out all of her privacy settings and hadn't accepted a single friend request. If anyone here saw it, they'd no doubt have questions. Like, why didn't she have any friends from her old school? Why wasn't she tagged in any photos? And why did she seem to have no past at all?

"I'll do it later," Ember said, her mind searching frantically for a way to change the topic. "You know what? I have something I've been meaning to ask you." She scrolled back through her camera all the way to the homecoming shots and found the photo of Claire and Ryan dancing. She pointed to the kid in the background. "Do you know this guy?"

Claire nodded. "That's Tommy Walker. He works tech crew."

"What do you know about him?"

Claire shrugged. "He's a sophomore. Super smart, but kind of weird. Knows what he's doing when it comes to lighting and sound, though." She looked at Ember. "Why? How do you know him?"

Ember hesitated. She should keep her mouth shut. She didn't need to be a witness to another crime, and she certainly didn't need to be nark-ing out the one person in Boyd County who knew her real identity and could expose her at any time. Still, a part of her wanted to confide in Claire. She was so sick of lying, of pretending, of keeping secrets.

"Ember, are you okay?" Claire reached out and touched her arm.

Ember grabbed her hand and held it. "If I tell you something, will you promise not to tell anyone?"

Claire nodded, her eyes wide. "Of course."

"During the homecoming game, I saw something I shouldn't have. Under the bleachers."

Claire drew back. "You mean … Tommy Walker?"

"Yeah."

Claire jumped up and plugged her ears. "Ew, gross. Don't tell me. I don't want to hear it. Ew, ew, ew." She grabbed Ember's shoulders. "I realize you can never un-see that, but you have to try to forget. Understand?"

Ember laughed and nodded. Claire had the wrong idea—a very, very wrong idea—but something about her reaction, her sweetness, her innocence, snapped Ember back to reality. No way could she confide in this girl. That huge ball of lies, pretending, and secrets she was living formed the entire basis of their friendship. If that ball started to unravel, if Claire knew who she really was and what she was really like, it would all be over.

# CHAPTER NINETEEN

*Five weeks earlier*

A shout woke her. It took Emily a moment to get her bearings. The tequila, the warmth of the fire, the soft strumming of the guitar must have lulled her to sleep. She stood and stretched as she walked toward a growing crowd down by the water. What was going on? How long had she been out? She searched for Zach, but it was so dark.

A loud wail rose from the crowd, sending a chill up her spine. A girl rushed by shouting into her cell phone. "Send an ambulance! We're on the shore, down by the pier."

An ambulance? That couldn't be good. Maybe someone had broken a leg playing volleyball, or maybe there'd been a fight. What if the cops showed up and started doing sobriety tests, and … Zach. Where was Zach? Emily took off in a run. *Please, please, please let Zach be okay.* Pushing her way through the crowd, she found him and Jimmy bent over someone. *Oh, thank God. He's safe.*

She took a deep breath and crept around them. What she saw would remain forever etched in her memory. It was Rosa, her hair and clothes sopping wet, her eyes lifeless, her lips a grayish blue.

"Breathe, damn it, breathe!" Zach pumped her chest while Jimmy performed mouth-to-mouth.

Emily let out a low moan. This couldn't be happening. She was talking to her just a few minutes ago. Well, the girl had been talking. Emily hadn't said much. She'd wanted to be left alone. She'd closed her eyes and turned away.

And now … this. Maybe if she'd been friendlier, if she'd reached out to her, paid attention, stayed awake. Then again, Rosa had brought up Emily's least favorite subject: Jimmy. And not just Jimmy, but *kissing* Jimmy. Ugh.

Emily stared as the girl's chest moved up and down with each breath Jimmy forced into her. But that was all it was. Forced air. Anyone could tell she would never draw another breath on her own.

Jimmy pulled away and cursed. The panicked look in his eyes triggered an alarm in Emily's head—an alarm much like the one that had sounded the morning after Molly's party. Something was off. Something had been off then, and something was off now, she could feel it.

What if?

Emily pushed her way back through the growing crowd and tore up the shore toward the bonfire. She vaguely remembered stepping over Rosa's half-full cup of beer when she woke. As she approached the fire, she saw the red cup, nestled neatly in the sand. She grabbed it and smelled it, then poured a little into her hand. It was a murky blue. A chill came over her despite the flames, and she crouched down, spitting up a putrid mixture of tequila and bile and fury.

"Give me that!" Brad Wahl appeared out of the darkness and snatched the cup out of her hand. "Mind your own business, Slutkowski." And with that, he threw the beer into the fire, where the evidence of "something being off" shot up into a brief, bright blaze of glory.

# CHAPTER TWENTY

Ember closed the door to the *Bulletin* office and raced to a desk in the back of the room. Her phone had beeped halfway through her last class, and she was dying to check it. It had to be Zach. He hadn't messaged her in almost a week. For the past half hour, she'd imagined a hundred possible DMs, ranging from "I will love you until my last breath," to "It's over and I never want to speak to you again." She closed her eyes and murmured a small prayer before looking at her screen.

Zach: This is bad. U need to make it stop.

What the ... Make what stop? Of all the messages

she'd imagined, this was not one of them. Was Zach being harassed? Would the mob try to get to her through him? Her hands shook as she messaged back.

Ember: What's going

"Hey. What are you up to?"

Ember shot out of her chair, dropping her phone. It clattered across the floor and skidded straight into Charles's well-worn cowboy boots.

He held his hands up in the universal don't-blame-me sign. "Sorry. Didn't mean to startle you."

He reached down to pick up the phone, but she practically pushed him out of the way as she dove to grab it first. "I got it."

Charles backed off. "Okaaay. Clearly I've intruded on something."

"No, it's nothing. It's … " Ember's voice caught. This was all too much. The constant lying. The hiding. Especially now, knowing that Zach might be in trouble despite her self-imposed exile—or maybe even because of it. And the worst part was, she knew the only way she'd find out for sure what was going on with him would be through a series of tortuous 140-character messages that he may or may not bother to return today, tomorrow, or even this week. She crumpled into her chair, and the tears started.

"Whoa, whoa." Charles crouched beside her.

"What's going on?"

Ember buried her face in her hands. "Nothing. I can't … " She broke down and sobbed. When she finally lifted her head, she was almost surprised to see Charles still crouched beside her. She wiped her eyes and met his gaze. "I need you to leave me alone."

"Ember, if you're in some sort of trouble … "

"No." She forced a smile. "No trouble. I'm a little homesick right now, that's all. I'll be okay."

He reached out and put his hand on her arm. "I'm sorry."

The tenderness of the gesture and the look of concern in his eyes were too much. The tears started again.

"Is there anything I can do?" he asked. "Besides leave you alone? Because I'm kind of not doing that."

Ember smiled in spite of herself, but she shook her head. There was nothing he or anyone could do.

"I have an idea. Something guaranteed to cheer you up." Charles pulled her out of her seat. "Come on. You can finish texting your friend on the way." He led her into the hallway and turned toward the exit.

"Where are we going?"

"The ranch."

"What ranch?"

"My ranch. I have something I want to show you."

Ember stopped.

"What's wrong?" Charles's eyes teased. "Never been to a farm before, city girl? I promise, the cows won't bite."

Ember stuck out her tongue. Charles was half right. She had never set foot on a farm before, but it wasn't the cows that scared her. It was her mother. If her mom found out, she'd be in huge trouble. She'd forbidden her from visiting anyone's house without her approval. Before she was allowed to stay at Claire's the other night, her mom had insisted on meeting both of her parents. Ember told her she was being overly protective, and even Deputy Steuben pointed out that their entire reason for moving here had been because it was such a safe community, but her mom was like a bear with cubs ever since the death threat. Go figure.

"Come on." Charles motioned to her to keep walking. "It'll be fun, you'll see."

"Can you get me back here by four? So my mom can pick me up?"

"Sure."

"Promise?"

He tipped a nonexistent cowboy hat. "Yes, ma'am."

Ember took a deep breath and followed him. She felt a fluttering in her stomach as she climbed into his truck, partly because she knew she was doing something she shouldn't, but also because she was curious to see Charles in his element. Despite the cowboy boots and the occasional piece of straw she noticed stuck to his jeans, she often had to remind herself that this tall, thin, bespectacled boy was a rancher. She couldn't imagine him riding a horse or lassoing a steer or whatever it was cowboy types did.

And she had tried to imagine it. More times than she cared to admit.

# CHAPTER TWENTY-ONE

The barn was dark and cavernous and smelled of sweet, dried hay. Ember paused inside the door to allow her eyes to adjust. Humongous rectangular bales lined one wall, stacked almost to the ceiling. The rest of the building was filled with tractors, tanks, wire fencing, and a bunch of machinery she couldn't begin to identify.

She hid her disappointment. She'd been hoping for animals—sheep and chickens and pigs—like in the storybooks and movies. Like in *Charlotte's Web*. This all seemed so … industrial.

"Up here." Charles scrambled up a steep set of stairs leading to a loft.

Ember hesitated. Was she crazy to follow him up there? After all, she didn't know him that well. What if under that sweet geek-boy exterior he was no different from Jimmy and Brad and their teammates? She hadn't seen another soul when they'd pulled in. Perhaps she was a lamb being led to slaughter.

Charles peered over the edge of the loft. "You coming? You're going to love this."

"What is it? Can you bring it down?"

"It's a surprise. And no." Charles's forehead creased, and he nodded toward the stairs. "You're not afraid of heights, are you?"

"No." Ember took a deep breath and climbed up. She stopped near the top of the staircase and peered around. The loft was empty except for a few scattered piles of hay. Charles sat in the far corner, a huge grin on his face. Her stomach clenched. He'd said he could "cheer her up." Was this what he had in mind—a literal roll in the hay? Was that how he thought of her?

Ember gripped the railing so hard her palms hurt. It was as though she had a blinking neon sign hanging over her head. "I'm Easy!" She'd thought she could leave the hot tub, the video, and her whole miserable sophomore year behind her, but maybe she couldn't. Not even halfway across the country. Not even with new hair, a new wardrobe, a new name. Maybe she was and always would be the Girl in the GIF, Emily Slutkowski.

Charles motioned for her to join him in the corner. She stood frozen, suspended between the desire to flee and the inevitability of giving in, as she had with all those other boys. Her eyes welled up. And that's when she heard it. A tiny, almost imperceptible cry. Something stirred in the hay behind Charles.

"What's that?"

He laughed. "Come see."

Ember practically flew up the final few steps and into the loft. She'd been wrong about Charles's intentions. Maybe even wrong about the neon sign.

He moved aside, revealing a writhing lump of fur nestled in the hay. Actually, upon closer inspection, Ember realized it was several lumps of fur. Kittens. Tiny black and orange and white kittens. "Aw. How cute." She knelt down and stroked one. It was so soft, so tiny. "How old are they?"

"Four days. Maybe five."

"Where's their mom?"

Charles glanced around. "Not far, I can promise you that. We'll have to move them soon, once they start walking." He nodded toward the ledge. "Wasn't very smart of her to have them up here." He scooped one up. It was orange with white paws and a white patch over one eye. "This little guy's my favorite. Calico Jack."

Ember reached over and grasped its tiny paw between her thumb and forefinger. "Calico? You do realize that makes no sense?"

"And why not?"

The glint in Charles's eyes told Ember she was walking into a trap, but she decided to go there anyway. "Because he's not a calico?"

"Aha! Right you are. But witness the patch and the boots. Calico Jack was the name of a famous pirate in the 1700s."

Pirate? Ember smiled. So Charles was a nerdy, strip-dancing, football-superhero, pirate-loving cowboy.

"Want to know what Calico was best known for?"

"What?"

"He had two women on his crew. Unthinkable in those days. They had to be seriously tough chicks."

Ember recalled his comment about her being tough after she'd taken the hit during her first assignment. "And you're into seriously tough chicks?"

He smiled. "Could be." He set the kitten down and began stroking the others. "Oh, no." His expression turned serious. "Crap."

"What's wrong?"

He gave her what had to be the most un-reassuring smile ever and shook his head. "Never mind."

"Never mind what? Tell me."

Charles's eyes held an apology, though she couldn't imagine why. "One is missing," he said finally.

"Missing? Oh, no. Did something get it? Like … " She scanned the rafters. "An owl?"

"No, not an owl."

"Then what? Oh, God." Ember jumped to her feet. "A snake? Do you have snakes?"

"No. It wasn't a snake." Charles looked away.

Ember felt a chill across the back of her neck. "Tell me. What happened to it?"

"You have to understand that six is kind of a big litter for a cat. That one was tiny, and—"

"What?" Ember backed away. She'd been rejected lots of times by lots of people, but never by her own mother. "No. No, no, no." She dropped to her knees and began crawling across the loft, rifling through the piles of hay.

"Ember." Charles's voice was barely louder than a whisper. "Don't."

"What do you mean, don't? We have to find it."

"You might not like what you find."

He was right, of course. She might be too late. But she had to try. When she'd finished scouring the loft, she climbed down the steps and scanned the barn. No way could she search this entire building. If the poor thing was even in here. If it had been brought outside, into the late-October chill, there would be no sense in looking.

Charles followed her down and rested his hand on her elbow. "It's okay. It's sad—horrible—but it happens. I'm … I'm sorry."

Ember wanted to pull away, or push him away, or scream at him and tell him it wasn't okay. She hated that being a rancher meant he could take this so casually, and she hated that she had romanticized ranching like some silly *Little House on the Prairie* fan girl. But that wasn't his fault. Besides, something about the way his voice caught when he said he was sorry told her that he was truly, terribly sorry. He'd brought her here to make her feel better and instead he'd given her a whole new reason to be upset.

She sighed and wiped away a tear that had crept into the corner of her eye. "This sucks." She turned away, and as she did, something caught her eye. Just a few feet away, under one of the tractors, two bright green eyes pierced through the dark.

Mama.

Ember walked over and bent down to glare at her. She was black and white and had a sweet face that gave no hint of the atrocity she'd committed.

"Where did you take it? Where's your baby?"

The cat bolted up the steps toward her litter.

"You'd better run," Ember shouted. "We're calling Kitty Protective Services on you!"

Charles cupped his hands around his mouth and hollered up into the loft. "Even better, we're having you spayed!"

Ember sagged against the tractor. "Not to state the obvious, but you should have done that a long time ago."

"Yeah, but she's not ours. I'm not sure whose she is. She just shows up every once in a while and hangs out in the barn." Charles walked over and kicked one of the tractor tires. "Kind of reminds me of you."

"Me?"

"Yeah. You showed up here, but I get the impression it's temporary. Or at least, you want it to be temporary."

He had that right. Ember was tempted to put her finger on her nose and shout, *Ding! Ding! Ding!* Instead, she shrugged. "Maybe. Maybe not. Anyway, what does it matter? We'll all be off at college in a couple of years, right?"

The kicking grew harder. So did Charles's voice. "Right."

"Why do you say it like that?"

He placed his boot on the hub of the tire and leaned into it. "College is a sore subject around here. My folks want me to go to agricultural school, but I want to study journalism."

"So what are you—"

Charles held up a hand. "Shh. Did you hear that?"

"Hear what?"

He dropped to his knees and peered under the tractor. "There it was again. Did you hear it?"

This time she did hear it. A tiny mewl. Her heart lifted. It had to be close by.

"I can't see it, but it sounds like it's right on the other side of this tire." Charles reached under and felt around but came up empty handed. The mewling grew louder.

Ember dropped to the ground and began to slither under.

"Whoa," Charles protested. "No you don't."

She peeked out. "I'll be in and out in five seconds, promise."

"Um. No. Crawling under a two-ton monster on wheels? Not happening."

The kitten meowed—whimpered, really—from just a couple of feet away. Ember ignored him and shimmied under to the inside of the tire. There in the wheel well sat the tiniest kitten she'd ever seen. She grabbed it and carefully backed up, inch by inch, her elbows scraping against the rough cement of the barn floor.

"Got him!" She rolled over and held the kitten up. It was black with a white belly, and it fit perfectly in the palm of her hand. Her elbows were bleeding, and she had grease in her hair, but she didn't care. "You're safe now, little guy." She sat up. "What should we name him?"

Charles gave her that same apologetic look. "Nothing. We're not naming him."

She rolled her eyes. "Right. Because farmers don't name their animals. Except you named Calico Jack, so how is this different?"

"Calico Jack is big and healthy. He'll be around for a while. This little guy needs to be handfed every two hours and kept warm and dry and out of trouble, and even then he probably only has a fifty-fifty chance of making it."

Ember's shoulders sagged. She hadn't thought about how they'd keep the kitten alive once they found it, but Charles was right. They couldn't exactly put it back up in the loft. Someone would have to take care of it. What would her mom say if she brought home a kitten? And not just any kitten, but one that needed to be nursed? She held it out to Charles. "Can you keep him?"

He shook his head. "We barely have enough manpower to take care of the cattle. No one's going to take a break every two hours to feed an undersized cat."

The kitten nudged Ember's thumb with its head. She kissed it lightly on one ear. No way was she giving up on this adorable creature. "Then I'll take him home. My mom can nurse him during the day, and I'll do it at night."

Charles reached over and stroked its teeny head. "Are you sure?"

"I'm sure."

"Promise not to name it, okay? Not for a few weeks."

"Too late. He's Oliver."

"As in Twist?"

"As in Twist."

Charles took Oliver from her and inspected its underside. "How do you know *he* isn't a *she*?"

Ember blinked. Why had she assumed the kitten was a boy? She shrugged. "If he turns out to be a girl, we'll call her Olivia."

"So if this little guy is Oliver Twist, does that make you Nancy?"

"Nancy? The hooker?" Nice. Ember grabbed Oliver out of Charles's hands and strode toward the door. "Screw you. Let's get out of here. I need to meet my mom."

"Hey, hey. That was a joke." Charles ran up and stood facing her, cutting off her exit. "Nancy may have been a prostitute, but she was also the purest soul in the novel." He leaned in, and his voice dropped. "And she was brave. She totally would have crawled under a tractor to save an orphaned kitten."

Ember's face reddened. "Not sure if that was bravery or stupidity."

"Doesn't matter. It was heart."

As the expression in Charles's eyes morphed from playful to serious and the hard line of his jaw softened, Ember felt something inside her slip away—the cage she used to contain herself here, and not just here, but back home, too. Before she knew what she was doing, she kissed him. It was a quick kiss at first, but then, when he didn't pull away, she kissed him again, a hard, determined kiss. Her head throbbed as she breathed him in, a combination of fresh hay and leather, so different from the beachy smell of …

She pulled away. Zach. Just a few hours ago he'd messaged her to let her know he was in trouble—his life possibly in danger because of her—and here she was kissing some other guy. What kind of girlfriend was she?

What kind of girl was she?

Charles stood still as a scarecrow, a dazed look on his face.

"I'm sorry." She turned and strode toward the exit. "Let's go."

"Sorry?" The sound of Charles's cowboy boots echoed sharply on the cement floor as he followed her. "What the hell? That was … "

"A mistake. Forget it."

He grabbed her arm, stopping her just inside the door. "You can't do that and then say forget it."

She pulled her arm away. "I just did." She tugged at the bar on the door, but it didn't budge. She'd need both hands and better leverage to open it—impossible since she was holding Oliver. She gritted her teeth. "Can I get some help here?"

Charles rested one hand on the bar. "As soon as you tell me what's going on. What was that about?" He sounded angry, hurt.

Ember studied his face. This was different. She was usually the one feeling used and confused. Had she caused that pain in his eyes? She looked away. "Like I said, it was a mistake. I'm sorry."

Charles said nothing. Ember focused on Oliver, petting him, whispering into his ear. "It'll be okay. Everything's going to be fine."

After a long few seconds, she heard the door slide and felt the cool rush of air on her face. She tucked the kitten to her chest, ran toward the truck, and leapt in. The ride back to school was long and filled with a stony silence.

# CHAPTER TWENTY-TWO

Ember was right about Zach not responding to her message for another week. Sort of. It took him four days, which was practically a week, and it felt like two.

Her phone buzzed partway through the first quarter of the Bruins' last home game of the season. She slipped under the bleachers to check it.

Zach: Coming home for Thanksgiving?

Ember sighed. He'd waited four days and then wrote *this*? First of all, Thanksgiving was a month away, and she hadn't started thinking about it yet. Second of all, no, she would not be going home. Did Zach not understand the concept of Witness Protection?

And third of all, this told her nothing. Nothing about how he was doing, nothing about how he was feeling, nothing about what he'd meant by his earlier plea to "make it stop." What was *it*?

"That your boyfriend?"

Ember started, almost dropping her phone. Tommy Walker was leering at her through the slats in the bleachers. She turned and walked away, but she could hear his feet clattering down the metal steps. Crap.

He caught up with her in seconds. "His name is Zach, right? How's he doing?"

A wave of nausea coursed through her. Tommy knew about Zach? Did he know what was going on back in Jersey? She turned and faced him. "What do you know about him?"

He sneered. "I know he's a senior at your old high school. I know he pitches for the baseball team. I know he is—or was—your boyfriend."

Ember waited for him to go on, but he seemed to have run out of fun facts. "That's it? That's all you know?"

Tommy hesitated. His left eye twitched. "Um. No. That's not all. I know lots of stuff."

"Like?"

"Like … " He pulled at his chin. "He has curly hair."

Ember breathed a sigh of relief. This guy knew more than he should—a lot more—but he didn't seem to have an inside scoop. Whoever he was, he wasn't Mafia. "Remember, we have a deal," she said. "You're keeping your mouth shut, right?"

He nodded. "You?"

"Yes. But I'll talk if you keep bothering me. In fact, the first person I'll tell is a certain deputy I know real well. Wouldn't that suck for you?"

Tommy took a step backward. "I'm not bothering you. I merely asked how your boyfriend's doing. Friendly conversation."

She glared. "He's fine, thanks. Now leave."

He turned to go, but wheeled back around. "Oh, yeah. One more thing I know about Zach." His sneer returned. "He has a new friend—chick named Allie. Very hot."

With that, he stalked away, leaving Ember to smolder. She studied the text again, then tucked her phone into her pocket without replying. Let Zach see how it felt to wait a few days.

\*\*\*

Ember tapped her foot and murmured at the computer. "Come on. I need to get out of here."

Her photos were taking forever to download, and she wanted to clear the *Bruins Bulletin* office before Charles arrived. She'd spoken exactly two words to him since The Kiss, a.k.a. The Mistake. She'd said, "Fine, thanks," after he'd asked how Oliver was doing. For the most part, she'd avoided him. He didn't seem to be seeking her out either.

When the "finished" window finally popped up, she unplugged her camera and whipped through the photos. She liked to tag her favorites to save Charles time when he reviewed and selected them. She'd snapped a great shot of a receiver making a one-handed grab and another of a Bruin running in the open field. When she reached the second-to-last photo, she stopped. That was by far the best one—Charles being hoisted into the air by his teammates. He'd kicked the game-winning field goal, a huge forty-two yarder, clinching the Bruins' spot in the state championship playoffs.

Ember studied his broad smile, his beautiful eyes, his victorious fist pump. She sighed. Mr. Football Superhero. Part of her was mortified she'd kissed him, but another part wanted to climb through the computer screen and kiss him all over again, this time softer, slower, sweeter.

"Whoa. Schmidt needs to watch his hand placement."

Ember jumped at the sound of Charles's voice behind her. "Would you quit doing that!"

"Doing what?"

"Sneaking up and startling me."

He ignored her distress, instead pointing to the bottom of the shot, where one of the linemen's hands hoisted Charles's thigh over his shoulder. "That looks obscene."

"No, it doesn't. It looks like he's picking you up and celebrating. Don't get all Marissa-y on me." Ember blushed, suddenly aware that she was talking to him. Using full sentences and multi-syllabic words. "Congratulations, by the way," she mumbled. "Nice kick."

"Thanks."

Ember grabbed her backpack to leave, but Charles bent down, his face—his highly kissable face—just a few inches from hers. "Let's see what else you got."

She scrolled back through the photos, pointing out the ones she'd tagged. Charles nodded in agreement, until she skipped past one of the cheerleaders doing lifts on the sidelines.

"Hold on. Go back to that one."

As soon as Ember clicked on it, she saw what

Charles had seen. Tommy Walker sitting on the bleachers in the background, sneering at the camera.

"What's with that guy?" Charles asked. "He's starting to creep *me* out."

"He's a loser. He's nobody."

"So you do know him?"

"Not really." Ember clicked to the next photo—a random shot of the bench—and pointed. "Check out this shot. I like the way these guys are … sitting."

Charles twirled her chair around so she faced him. The gentle expression in his eyes made her heart hurt. No guy—not even Zach—looked at her like that. "Ember, enough," he said. "Who is he? And why does he keep staring at you?"

Ember bit her lip. What if she told him? What if she spilled everything right now—who she was, where she was from, why she was here? End the whole charade. As good as it might feel to finally tell someone the truth, she knew she couldn't do it. First of all, it would compromise the program, putting herself, her mom, and Tricia at risk. Second, if Charles knew her real identity, it would probably take him about three minutes on Google to discover everything else about who she really was. Then he'd look at her the same way the guys back home did. She couldn't bear that.

She forced a smile. "Okay, you got me. I didn't

want to say anything, because … "

"Because what? What's going on?"

"This is so embarrassing." Ember ran her fingers through her cropped hair. "His name is Tommy Walker, and … " She dropped her voice even though they were the only ones in the office. "We had a thing."

"A thing?

"No, not really a thing. It was one date."

"With him?"

"Yeah. I know, it was stupid. Because he's creepy. But I was new, and I didn't know anyone, and … you can't say anything to anybody, okay? Especially not him. Let's just say it didn't go well."

"What happened?" Alarm registered in Charles's eyes.

"Oh, nothing. Nothing like that. He was fine, though not my type." She stood, backpack in hand. "Anyway, now it's over, and it's all good."

"Except for the staring."

She sighed. "I can handle the staring. I can handle Tommy Walker. Let it go, all right?"

Charles's eyes narrowed. She got the impression he didn't like to let things go. "Fine. But you have to answer one question."

"Okay."

"Last week, in the barn. Is that why you … you

know? Because you're new and you don't know anyone?"

Ember would have given anything to have the floor open up and swallow her and spit her back out in New Jersey, never to face Charles again, but she forced herself to stay calm, casual. "Pretty much. I'm full of stupid these days."

He let out a long breath. Disappointment or relief? "You're sure?" he asked.

"Positive."

"Got it."

She wheeled around and headed for the door. "Good."

# CHAPTER TWENTY-THREE

*Seven weeks earlier*

Emily collapsed onto her bed. Her first day back at school had gone better than she could have dreamed. Not only had the football goons stopped bothering her, they'd become perfect gentlemen— smiling at her in class, opening doors for her, saying "excuse me" if they happened to brush up against her in the crowded hallways.

It was almost as though they were afraid of her.

She grabbed the notebook sitting on her nightstand and reviewed her list one more time.

*Pros and Cons of Going to the Cops*

### PROS

*Jimmy gets what he deserves.*
*Justice for Rosa.*
*No more victims.*
*Trina.*

### CONS

*What if I have to testify?*
*What if no one believes me?*
*What if everyone totally hates me?*
*Trina.*

Trina was on both lists. She was on the "pro" list because Emily wanted more than anything to protect her. If she did nothing, said nothing, who would be next? Maybe it wouldn't happen again tomorrow, or next week, or even next year. Maybe it would be a few years from now. Sure, Jimmy d'Angelo would be gone by then, but there would be other guys to take his place. She could already see it in some of the freshmen who idolized him and his crowd.

On the other hand, she was also on the "con" list, because going to the cops would mean telling them about that night at Molly's. Emily was convinced she'd been drugged just like Rosa. It made so much sense. But digging that back up, making it public, would mean Trina would hear all about it and would most likely see the GIF. The thought made Emily sick to her stomach.

The front door closed and her mom's footsteps sounded on the stairs. Emily sat up and tucked the list under her pillow.

"Hey, sweetie. I brought home some Wok 'n' Roll for dinner."

She forced a smile. "Sounds great. Be right down."

Her mom. She couldn't even think about her seeing the GIF. Ugh.

"First dibs on the moo shu pork," her sister called as she slipped past her door.

"Hey! No, you don't." Emily jumped up and ran after her. Their mom never bought enough moo shu.

They ate sitting on the floor around the living room coffee table. Halfway through dinner, Trina set down her chopsticks. She'd been unusually quiet.

"Something wrong?" their mom asked.

Trina's face grew red. "This is so embarrassing."

Emily and her mom looked at each other.

"What is it, sweetie?"

"It started today."

"What started?"

Trina took another bite of her pork and rolled her eyes.

"Oh, sweetheart." Her mom's voice caught. "You're growing up so fast." She looked back and forth at the two of them. "You both are."

"Oh. *That* started." Emily smirked. "Lucky you."

Trina returned her smirk but then burst into tears.

"Oh my gosh, seriously?" Emily kicked her sister's shin. "It's not that big a deal, T. You'll see. Calm down."

Trina's sobbing grew louder. "I know. It's just … it makes you emotional, right?"

"I guess. But … emotional, not hysterical." Emily's amusement morphed into alarm as her sister's sobs grew stronger. What was going on? Trina could do moody, snarky, and sour like a boss, but she rarely cried. This was more than hormones. Emily could feel it. She scooted beside her. "What happened?"

"Nothing. It's stupid."

Their mom appeared with a box of tissues, and Emily wiped her sister's eyes. "Come on, T. Talk to me."

She shook her head. "I don't want to."

"Well, I'm not leaving you alone until you do."

Trina grabbed a tissue and blew her nose. "Whatever." She gave their mom a no-way-am-I-telling-you look.

Their mom grabbed a fortune cookie and headed toward the staircase. "I get it. You two clean up the dishes when you're done."

Trina fingered her napkin, waiting until their mother was out of earshot. "Remember when you said high school wasn't all rainbows and butterflies? Well, neither is eighth grade."

Emily nodded. Sometimes, with all she'd gone through the past year, she'd forgotten how hard middle school could be. "Tell me, T. Promise I'll understand."

Trina plucked a tissue out of the box and buried her face in her hands. "It's humiliating."

Emily put her arm around her. "Shh. It's okay."

They sat in silence for a long time, Trina crying and Emily rubbing her back. Finally, she spoke again. "I noticed it right before gym, and I kind of freaked out. I had to ask Ms. Martin for a pad."

"Awkward."

"I know, right? And Ms. Martin gets all excited and starts saying, 'Oh, your first period … so exciting … rite of passage … blah, blah, blah.' And then Callie Malone overhears us, and she starts telling everyone. And the next thing I know, somebody tapes that stupid picture of me with the kite up on my locker with a huge red magic marker streak going across it."

"Your gym locker?"

"No, my *locker* locker. Like, in the middle of D Hall where everyone in the whole school probably saw it." Trina grabbed more tissues and cried into them.

Emily felt the same sense of nausea she'd had when she first watched the infamous GIF on her phone. She pulled Trina into her chest and rocked her. "I'm sorry, T. People suck. They really do."

"I know." Trina hiccupped. "Brie and Cece have been nice about it, but the A-Crowd all act like it's a huge joke. Jon Kripps started calling me Bloodkowski."

Tears pricked Emily's eyes. She wanted so badly to tell her sister to ignore those stupid kids, that the teasing was silly and things would get better. But how could she? She was living proof that things could get worse. In fact, if she went to the police about Rosa's death, things could get much worse. Not just for her, but for Trina too. The whole town could see that GIF.

"Some people look for reasons to be mean," she said. "At least getting your period's not your fault."

"What do you mean by that?"

Emily looked her sister in the eye. "It means you walk into the school tomorrow with your head up, and you tell those stupid A-Listers that—"

"A-Crowd."

"Whatever. You tell them you have no time for

their immature stunts."

"Good idea. Except maybe I should say 'shenanigans' instead. While wagging my finger at them." Trina gave her a hug. "Thanks, sis. You've been incredibly un-helpful."

Emily smiled. This was the Trina she knew and loved. "Any time."

Maybe everything would be okay. No doubt the middle school bullies would forget about her sister and move on to the next poor kid tomorrow.

Trina grabbed the fortune cookies and held them out. "Pick one."

"You can pick first tonight."

Trina selected hers and cracked it open. "*You love Chinese food.*" She shook her head. "Hilarious. What does yours say?"

Emily opened her cookie and tugged at the fortune inside. Her stomach rolled as she read it.

*Be the change you seek.*

# CHAPTER TWENTY-FOUR

"Oh my gosh. He is sooo cute!" Claire grabbed Ember's phone and passed it to Marissa. "You have to see this."

Marissa set down her pear and watched the video. Ember expected her to roll her eyes or sneer or shrug, but to her surprise, Marissa smiled. "He's adorable … and so tiny. Look at him chasing his tail."

"If you think he's little now, you should have seen him when I first got him. I swear he's doubled in size already."

"Where did you say you found him again?"

Ember stared down at her tray and began rearranging the mushroom slices on her pizza. She hadn't told anyone about her visit to Charles's barn. Aside from finding Oliver, she wished the whole thing had never happened. "Sitting on the side of the road. Abandoned and scared."

Ember sat with Claire, Marissa, and their table full of friends every day at lunch now. Considering that they'd all gone to school together since kindergarten, she knew they'd always think of her as the "new girl," but some days she almost felt like she fit in, like she could belong. She took a sip of her soda and changed the subject toward something she knew the rest of the girls would appreciate. "So, the state playoffs. What will that be like?"

Marissa grinned. "No idea. BCHS hasn't been there since, like, the '80s. It'll be fun to go on the road, though."

"I can't wait." Claire said. "You'll be on the bus too, right? As the official team photographer?"

The pizza churned in Ember's stomach. Six hours in a bus full of football players? Ugh. Much as she reminded herself, over and over, that things were different here, certain images haunted her. "I guess."

"Speaking of photography, I love this picture of the guys celebrating." One of the girls, a tall, quiet brunette named Suzette, opened a copy of the *Bulletin* to the sports page with the shot of Charles. She leaned in, lowered her voice, and pointed to the photo. "Did you notice this, though? Marcus Schmidt's hand is practically in his crotch."

Ember laughed. "Please don't let Charles hear you say that. I told him no one would notice."

"It was the first thing I noticed," Marissa said.

Of course. With her photographer's eye and all.

"What I don't understand is how Marcus can even play," Claire said. "I keep expecting him to get kicked off the team, but he's out there every Friday."

"What do you mean?" Ember asked.

"You can't do sports if you're failing, and he failed English the first quarter."

"How do you know that?"

"I sit beside him. Trust me, he failed."

Ember shrugged. "Maybe they let him do some makeup work. He's one of the players Coach Sebastian kept telling me is critical for the defense."

"That would be so unfair." Claire pouted. "I got a B, and when I asked whether I could do anything to bring it up, Ms. Gerard said, 'I suppose you could study more next quarter.'"

Marissa shook her head. "Wow. She is such a wench."

"I know, right?"

"Don't worry. I'm pretty sure one B won't keep

you out of NYU." Marissa grabbed the paper from Suzette and held it up as though she were reviewing Claire's college application. "Well, she's taking all AP classes, has a 4.3 GPA, starred in every high school play, not to mention every grade school production since the fourth grade, cheered all four years of high school, and ... uh, oh. What's this B in her first quarter English class her junior year? Hmm ... "

" ... next!" Ember shouted.

Marissa laughed and gave Ember a fist bump.

"Seriously, Claire," Suzette said. "If you can't get into any college you want, the rest of us should drop out and start flipping burgers now."

The bell rang and Ember grabbed her tray. As she stood, a slight waving motion a few tables away caught her eye. Tommy Walker was staring at her. He had a huge grin on his face and was doing something weird with his hand—almost like he was conducting music, but with a bent wrist. What was that about? She turned and headed toward the exit. The last thing she needed was for him to bother her here, in front of her new friends.

As she deposited her lunch tray on the counter, it hit her. His hand. He was making the exact same motion she'd made as she dangled Molly's bikini top in the air.

He'd seen the GIF.

# CHAPTER TWENTY-FIVE

Playing hard to get worked. When she finally messaged Zach back, he responded right away.

    Zach: Where u been? Missed u! <3 <3 <3

She crumpled onto her bed and held her phone to her cheek. She missed him, too. She closed her eyes and recalled the first time he kissed her, that late spring evening under the pier. She'd wanted so badly all evening to feel his arms around her and to run her hands along his beautiful chest and shoulders, but when he finally made his move, it didn't work out that way. Partly because he was a total gentleman and partly because that silly stuffed flamingo kept getting in the way.

Ember smiled at the memory. She'd felt the soft sand beneath her feet and breathed in the hundred years' worth of salt water that permeated the pylons. Her heart was pounding so hard she was sure Zach could hear it over the roar of the waves. He'd brushed her hair away, pretending to want a closer look at her ear cuff, but then he'd lightly stroked her ear, her neck, her shoulder, finally pulling her toward him and kissing her. His lips were softer than she'd imagined, and they tasted like a mixture of sea salt and cotton candy. And all of that was amazing, but none of it was her favorite part of the kiss.

Her favorite part was what he'd said afterward. He caressed her lips with his thumb and said, "I've wanted to do that for a long time, but I haven't had the nerve. Think we can do it again sometime?"

So sweet, and nothing at all like the way the other boys talked to her.

She missed Zach, she missed the shore, and crazy as it seemed, part of her even missed those other boys and everyone who'd made her life so miserable for the past year. At least they knew exactly who she was and what she was. Here her whole life was a lie. Yes, she had some friends, but all it would take would be for Tommy Walker to share that GIF with them and her fragile little social circle would wash away faster than a sandcastle at high tide.

Without thinking—or more accurately, without letting herself think—she dialed the phone. She wanted to hear Zach's voice, needed to hear it. He was the only person in the entire world who knew everything about her and loved her anyway.

"Hello? Hello?" Zach paused, then lowered his voice. "Em, is that you?"

She hung up. Crap. She shouldn't have done that. Of course, he would guess it was her. He'd messaged her two minutes ago. And now he had her phone number. He knew the area code and everything. Crap, crap, crap.

She closed her eyes. She didn't care. It was worth it. Hearing his voice—the Jersey accent mellowed by his surf-boy vibe—was worth whatever happened next. And probably, nothing would happen next. She messaged him back.

Ember: <3 u 2. Delete that number. I could get in big trouble.

She stared at the Twitter icon on her phone, willing it to light up. After a minute, it did.

Zach: U got it. Wish u'd said hi. Miss ur voice.

Ember's eyes welled. She didn't belong in Boyd

County. She belonged back in Jersey with Zach. She needed to focus on getting home, testifying, and finding a way to put this whole mess behind her.

\*\*\*

Ember awoke with a start. How embarrassing. She'd fallen asleep on the team bus. She straightened and wiped at her chin. At least she wasn't drooling. She peered around. A bunch of the kids had dozed off. It was one a.m. after all, and they'd been riding for almost five hours. Beside her Claire clicked away at Candy Crush on her phone, and across from her Charles had his eyes closed, but his left hand kept time to the song piping through his earbuds.

Ember stretched. The french fries from their ten p.m. snack stop felt heavy in her stomach, and her back ached from the hard bus seats. Still, she had to admit it had been a fun ride.

She'd been dreading it all week, but when she boarded the bus, she was relieved to find that Claire had saved a seat for her. She'd tucked her camera case carefully under her seat and scoped out the scene.

The bus was about half full at that point, with

cheerleaders and players sitting mixed together. A feeling of excitement and anticipation filled the air. This was their first overnight trip, and a win in tomorrow's semi-final would mean a spot in the state championship game.

Charles hadn't boarded yet—not that Ember cared. She eyed the empty seat across from her. No, she was being stupid. Charles could sit wherever he wanted. It made no difference to her. She loved Zach, adored him, needed him, missed him so badly she could feel it in her bones.

So what was up with the butterflies when Charles flopped down across from her?

"Hey there, cat whisperer. How's Ollie doing?"

Ember laughed. "He's adorable. Though I should have named him Dr. Jekyll. One minute he's snuggled up in my lap, purring away, and the next he's tearing through the house like some sort of whirling dervish."

Claire leaned toward them. "Do you still have the video? You have to show him the video."

Ember took out her phone and searched for it as Claire proceeded to describe the whole thing to him anyway. Ember tensed. What if she mentioned something about Oliver being found on the side of the road? Or if Charles brought up the barn? Finally, she found it.

"Here we go." She handed it to Charles. "That was almost a week ago, so he's even bigger now."

Charles whistled. "Impressive. I think he's outgrown the rest of the litter."

Ember froze. Crap. Why did he have to say that? She could feel Claire staring at them.

"Speaking of … " Charles said. "Do you want to adopt them, too? They're driving my dad crazy. Running all over the—"

"You should see the trick I taught him," Ember interrupted. "He can fetch."

"Fetch? Like a dog?"

"Yeah. His little kitty toys. He brings them back and everything." She bit her lip and glanced at Claire. She was watching them with a slight smile and raised eyebrows, but she said nothing.

Ember felt herself relax. Claire had the wrong idea—well, she had the right idea, though probably a sweeter, more romantic version of it—but Ember could trust her to keep quiet.

"I've never heard of a cat playing fetch before. Maybe you really are a cat whisperer." Charles leaned across the aisle, and his voice dropped. "It's those green eyes. They'd charm any cat. Heck, they'd charm a great white shark."

Ember had blushed when he'd said it, and she

blushed now as she remembered it. Thank goodness the lighting was so dim and Claire was absorbed in her game.

Charles had noticed her eyes. And he found them charming.

Ember sighed and laid her head back in her seat. She started to drift off again, a reluctant smile teasing her lips, when something drew her out of her haze. Two players were whispering behind her—arguing—and she could swear she heard the word, "Walker."

She held her breath and listened.

"We took care of it," one of them was saying. "Let it go."

"Punk cannot keep a secret. He needs to learn to keep his mouth shut, or Imma shut it for him."

"He will. We taught him his lesson. Trust me, he's solid. And anyway, he has as much to lose now as you do."

Ember drew her legs up to her chest and hugged them. Her first thought was that they were somehow talking about her, about her secrets, about the GIF. But that made no sense. No, this must be about the drug deal. And maybe it wasn't the kinds of drugs she'd imagined. Maybe Tommy Walker was dealing steroids, and the coach was giving them to his players. His best-ever defense. That made a lot of sense.

Not that Ember cared. She still had no interest in becoming a witness to another crime. And steroids weren't even a crime, were they? More like breaking the rules. Whatever. It meant nothing to her.

On the other hand, the fact that Tommy Walker couldn't keep secrets? That meant something.

# CHAPTER TWENTY-SIX

Ember frowned. Her photos were all overexposed. This was the first time she'd shot an afternoon game since homecoming, and that had been a cloudy day. Today the sun shined so brightly she had to squint even through her camera lens. The opponents' dark uniforms and helmets showed up fine, but the Bruins players, in their white jerseys, looked like a team of ghosts.

That was the problem with overexposure. It washed everything out—the fine lines, the subtle shadows, the delicate textures. Only the dark parts stood out. The same thing had happened to her. After Molly's party, after her "overexposure," it was as though everything good about her had faded to nothing. Her easy laugh, her solid grades, her killer photography skills—everything that made her Emily Slovkowski became washed out, leaving the dark stain of that night as her entire identity.

Until Zach came along. Zach treated her like a normal human being. He reminded her of who she'd been, and who she could be. She couldn't forget that. She had to do whatever it took to get back to him.

"Having problems?" Marissa's voice startled her. It was halftime, and the other team's cheerleaders had taken the field.

"No. What do you mean, 'problems'?"

Marissa shrugged. "You're staring at your viewfinder and practically growling." She reached for the camera.

Ember tucked it under her arm. "It's no big deal. A few minor exposure issues. I just need to adjust my shutter speed."

"That sun is wicked. You might want to check your F-stops, too."

Seriously? As if she wouldn't know to check her F-stops? Ember had the urge to ask Marissa whether any of her work had ever been featured on the cover of a professional photography magazine, but of course she couldn't. She gritted her teeth. "Will do."

Marissa tilted her head up and shielded her eyes.

"Have you ever taken photos at the beach?"

Ember hesitated. Had she read her mind? Had she seen the photo of her sister flying the kite and started to piece things together? "I guess," she said finally. "Why?"

"I've only been to the beach once in my life." Marissa had a faraway look in her eyes. "A few years ago, we flew to California to go to Disneyland and then drove to LA for a couple of days. Hardest place in the world to take photos—all that sand reflecting the sun. Until it started to set. But even that sucked, because there's no way in the world to capture the beauty of a Santa Monica sunset on film."

Ember nodded. She'd never seen the sun set on the water, but she'd seen lots of Atlantic coast sunrises, and she knew exactly what Marissa meant. "Some things have to be witnessed live."

"Exactly." Marissa sighed and waved a pompom at her. "Gotta run. Our squad's up next."

*Bzzz.* Ember's phone vibrated in her back pocket. She smiled. All week long, Zach had been sending her daily messages, each one sweeter than the last.

```
Zach: Thinking of you
Zach: Miss your beautiful face
Zach: Can't wait to be together
again.
```

He really did miss her as much as she missed him.

She slipped away to the corner of the field and scrolled through her account. He always said weekends were hardest for him. She held her breath as she clicked on the Twitter icon. What would today's message be?

`Zach: Hey slut! Why r u sending messages to my bf? Stay away.`

Ember's blood ran cold. *What the* … Someone must have hacked into Zach's account.

Unless … oh, no. Please. No, no, no. Tears sprang to her eyes, and her hands began to shake. Surfgurrl. Could she be on his phone right now? She imagined the sweet face that peered over his shoulder in the photo sending this hateful note. Why would she do such a thing? Why would Zach hang out with someone like her? And why, why, why was she calling him her boyfriend?

# CHAPTER TWENTY-SEVEN

"We have a problem." Deputy Steuben stepped past Ember into the living room before she even had a chance to invite him in.

"What is it?" Tricia looked up from her book report.

Their mom appeared from the kitchen, her left cheek streaked with flour and her hair pinned back into a loose bun. She was in full fall pie baking mode. "Yes, what is it?"

"We appear to have a breach." He gaze met Ember's. "An internal breach."

Oh, no. Ember sank into the nearest chair. This could be bad. Really bad.

Her mom turned toward her, her face almost as

pale as the streak of flour. "What does that mean? How can that be?"

Ember held up her hands, motioning for her mother to calm down. "Mom, it's no big deal. It's just Zach, and it's not like he has my address or—"

"No contact!" Her mother's voice ranged somewhere between a bark and a shriek. "What part of 'no contact' did you not understand?"

Ember shrank back into the cushions. She wasn't used to seeing her mom angry. Worried, yes. It seemed she was constantly worrying. But not angry. She opened her mouth, but nothing came out. How could she explain? She needed Zach like she needed food and air. She needed to know and believe there was one person in this world who knew exactly who she was and loved her anyway. But she couldn't tell her mom that. Especially not now, when she wasn't even sure it was still true. Zach hadn't sent her a single message since that horrible punch in the gut she'd received at Saturday's game. She had no idea what was going on, and she wasn't sure she wanted to.

"So what now?" Her mom turned toward the deputy. "What do we do?"

Deputy Steuben walked over to Ember and held out his hand. "First things first. Your phone."

"Wait. Really?" Ember knew she should keep her

mouth shut but … crap. Her phone? She glanced at her mom, but she clearly wasn't getting any sympathy from her.

"Don't worry. You'll get it back." Deputy Steuben waited, his hand still outstretched.

Ember reached into her pocket. She hesitated. This couldn't be good, but she had no choice. She handed it over and bit her lip.

He stuck the phone in his front shirt pocket. "Thank you. Next, we need to—"

"When will I get it back?"

"Excuse me?"

"You said I'd get it back." She was pushing it, but she needed to know. "When?"

Deputy Steuben rubbed his eyes. "You know, when I was your age, I didn't even have a phone. We couldn't afford it. Even all through college, all I had was a flip phone. You'll live. But if you must know, it'll be two or three days, depending on how many messages you have."

"Meaning you're going to read my messages?"

He glared. When he finally answered, his voice was hard. "Actually, I'm going to have an admin transcribe them. Then I'm going to read them. And then I'm going to delete your account." He paused as if to let that sink in. "They're all through Twitter, right? You didn't contact him or anyone else through any other accounts?"

Ember shook her head, fighting back tears. So some faceless administrative assistant and Deputy Steuben and who knew how many other people from the U.S. Marshals Service were going to read her messages. It was so unfair, so stupid. Those messages were private. They would mean nothing to anyone but her and Zach. She took a deep breath. She would not let them see her cry.

Her mom spoke up. "So, you were about to say— next we need to … what?"

"Well, to some extent, that depends on the messages." He patted his pocket. "If in fact the only person Ember has contacted is Zach and his messages to her raise no threat, we don't do much. I'll have to step up my surveillance of your house, meaning you'll be seeing me twice a week instead of once, and we'll keep a closer eye on a certain witness to make sure she doesn't do anything like this again." He paused and gave Ember a pointed stare.

She studied his sneakers. She should tell him about the last message, the one from surfgurrl. He was going to find out about it anyway. But how could she in front of her mom and Tricia? By now, that message had been etched into her brain and burned onto her eyeballs.

She hadn't been called "slut" in so long, she'd almost forgotten how it felt.

"Anything you need to tell me?" Deputy Steuben asked. "Speak now or forever hold your peace."

Ember glanced at her mom and sister. "Can we talk outside?"

Deputy Steuben's eyebrows shot up. He stood, shook her mom's hand, and motioned for Ember to follow him. He led her out to his car, stopped, and leaned against it. "What's up?"

"The last message. You should read it."

Deputy Steuben retrieved the phone from his pocket and tapped through to her Twitter account.

Ember kicked one of his tires. "It's not from him. I mean, it's Zach's account, but he didn't write it. No way. I think it was this girl he's been hanging out with."

"I see." He scowled and his eyes flashed with anger.

Ember braced herself. Here it came, and she supposed she deserved it. She'd broken the number one rule of Witness Protection. But when Deputy Steuben spoke, his voice was soft, kind. "They're just words, you know."

"What?" She blinked.

He pointed to her screen. "Sticks and stones and all that. Ignore it."

Ember snorted. "Right. I don't care if people make

fun of me ... said no one, ever. At least, not honestly."

"Yeah, well, screw 'em. You're better than that. You're one of the good guys, Ember. Don't forget it."

Ember turned and wiped her eyes. She refused to cry in front of him. Anyway, he had to say those things. He was being paid to take care of her, to make sure she kept her promise and took the stand next month. "So, what now? Am I in bigger trouble because of ... her? I mean, it's not like she knows where I am or anything. And her message is hardly a threat to come after me. In fact, she's telling me to stay away."

"We'll see." Deputy Steuben opened his car door and slid in behind the wheel. "I'll have the Jersey office look into her. Probably not a big deal." He shut the door and rolled down his window. "Stay out of trouble, okay?"

Ember nodded. She turned to walk away, but then turned back around. "By the way, how'd you find out about all this?"

Steuben gave her a wry grin. "The phone call."

Ember's eyes widened. "Oh my gosh. I completely forgot about that."

"Did you also forget who owns the phone? Who do you think pays your bill?"

Of course. She'd never even thought about it. But in that case, shouldn't they have known earlier? "So wait. You didn't find out until you got the bill?"

Deputy Steuben scowled. "The call should have been flagged as soon as you made it, but the idiots over in tech never caught it. Fortunately some of the folks in accounting have their heads screwed on straight. First thing we did was grab your buddy's phone. Mysteriously disappeared from his pocket a few hours ago while he was eating lunch at a hotdog stand on the boardwalk."

"Did it still have my number stored? Because I told him to delete it. He said he deleted it."

Deputy Steuben shook his head. "It was clean."

She gave a sigh of relief. Zach had at least taken that seriously.

"Remember, we're doing all this for a reason. It's not just to torture you."

"I know. I haven't forgotten." She waved goodbye and watched as he pulled away.

How could she forget?

# CHAPTER TWENTY-EIGHT

*Nine weeks earlier*

Emily fluffed the bow on the little girl's dress and peered into her huge brown eyes. "What's your name?"

"Manta."

Her mother laughed. "It's Samantha."

"Beautiful name for a beautiful child."

Her mom and dad beamed. They were a beautiful family. Emily congratulated herself on picking out the perfect cowboy hat for the dad. She could tell he loved it. If she played her cards right, she might make a premium package sale and a nice little commission.

"I'm Emily, by the way." She held out her hand.

"Dominic. And this is my wife, Jen." He shook her

hand and tipped his hat.

Emily smiled. "You know, you sort of remind me of a young Clint Eastwood in that." They all wanted to be Clint Eastwood.

He squinted and placed his hand on his holster. "Go ahead. Make my day."

Emily laughed. Oh, yeah. Easy sale.

For the first set of shots she posed Samantha on her dad's lap, with her mom standing behind them. She could tell by the way Dominic smoothed his daughter's hair and tickled her legs and fussed over her that he was a great dad.

Had her own father treated her like that? She couldn't remember. He'd split when she was seven, and most of her memories consisted of him being passed out drunk on the couch or fighting with her mom about bills. Still, there must have been a time when her mom and dad were happy and in love. Maybe when she was Samantha's age he did fuss over her.

Sure enough, once Dominic saw the shots, he sprang for the premium package. He paid in cash and even threw in a twenty-dollar tip. "You do good work."

"Thanks. I'm planning to study photography in college."

"If you make it to college." He smiled and waved as he followed his wife and Samantha toward the exit.

What was that supposed to mean? Did she seem like the kind of girl who couldn't get into college? Emily shook her head and headed into the changing room. She heard the *Bzz-Bzz* of the door as they left.

Seriously, what a weird thing for him to say. She could still feel the pressure of his hand as he placed the money in her palm, but now, instead of making her grin, it gave her the creeps. Something was off. She picked up the brown suede shirt he'd worn and hung it on the rack. As she began buttoning it, a noise startled her.

She turned to find Dominic standing behind her. His face was hard and cold, nothing like the sweet father she'd just photographed. She reached for a nearby parasol, but he grabbed her wrist.

"You might want to check the pocket."

"What?" Her voice came out as a yelp.

He nodded toward the shirt. "I may have left something in the pocket." Just as quickly as he appeared, Dominic was gone.

Emily's knees felt weak, and she had to sit down on the bench against the wall. Her mind flashed to a scene that had played out that day at school. She was in the cafeteria, getting some juice out of the vending machine, when someone bumped into her hard from behind. She'd turned to find Jimmy d'Angelo glaring at her. "Sorry," he said. "I didn't see you standing there."

His glare sent a shiver up her spine. Should she tell someone? Her mom? The cops? No. Jimmy was a jerk, that was all. The police had promised confidentiality when she's called them the night before and told them about Rosa's blue beer. No way did he know she'd talked.

But Dominic's glare held a threat, and now she felt certain Jimmy's had too. Crap. As if she didn't have enough trust issues, now she couldn't even trust the cops.

She took a deep breath. Dominic had said to check his pocket. She grabbed the shirt. Its only pocket was on the front right. She noticed a slight bulge, and her hands shook so badly it took her several tries to unbutton it. Inside she found a neatly folded piece of paper. It looked vaguely familiar.

Emily slowly peeled it open. When she saw the image, she shrieked and dropped it. *No, no, no. Please, God, no.*

# CHAPTER TWENTY-NINE

"I 'll have a venti hazelnut latte." Ember paid for her coffee and made her way over to her friends' table.

The Starbucks in the grocery store was a poor substitute for the coffee shops back home, but it felt good to be out of the house. She'd been stuck inside with no phone since Saturday. They had Monday and Tuesday off for Veterans Day and a teachers' in service day.

"Lamest long weekend ever." She set her cup down next to Claire's.

"Why didn't you tell me you lost your phone?"

"Well, if someone would check her email … "

"Who checks email?"

"How else was I supposed to tell you?"

"Ever heard of Twitter? Facebook?" Marissa butted in.

"Ember doesn't do social media, remember?" Claire ripped open at least five packets of sugar and poured them into her coffee. "My gosh. Four days without a phone. I'd die. You're getting another one, right?"

"Of course. Not sure when it'll get here, though. Maybe not for another few days."

"That's weird." Marissa's eyes narrowed. "When I broke my old phone, my new one arrived practically the next day."

Ember took a sip of her coffee. Why did she always have to be such a know-it-all? "Yeah, well, with the holiday and all … " She stood up. "Can you guys watch my cup for a minute? I'm going to buy some gum."

She headed over to the checkout counters. She did want gum, but mostly she wanted to stop talking about her phone. Next thing she knew, Marissa would grill her about how she lost it, where she last saw it, who she'd called or texted, and on and on. She was getting tired of the lies, and Deputy Steuben was right. She needed to be careful. She was doing all of this for a reason, a very good reason.

She closed her eyes and forced herself to remember. The *PhotoPro* cover of her sister flying her kite had been stuffed into the shirt pocket that day in the Shoot 'Em Up. It was a shot she'd admired a hundred times, only on this copy someone had meticulously drawn a bullet hole through the middle of her sister's forehead. She'd immediately dialed Trina and her mom. When neither of them answered their phones, she ran all the way home, panicked and desperate. When she found them in the kitchen blithely cooking up a pot of spaghetti sauce with Justin Timberlake blaring on the stereo, she hugged her sister so hard she knocked the breath out of her. Later that night, when she showed her mom the photo, it took about two minutes for her mother to get the U.S. Marshals on the phone.

"You can't go wrong with wintergreen, you know."

Ember opened her eyes to find Charles standing on the other side of the candy rack, a bemused smile on his face. Her cheeks grew warm. How long had she been standing there? And how long had he been watching? "Hi," she said. "What are you doing here?"

He laughed, a warm, teasing laugh. "Trust me. You stand in the checkout lane at Super Saver long enough, you'll run into everyone in Boyd County."

Ember grabbed a pack of wintergreen—because it was her favorite, not because he'd suggested it—and got in line. She waved toward the Starbucks. "I'm having coffee with Claire and Marissa and some others. Want to join us?"

Charles picked up a packet of Skittles and fell in line behind her. "Actually, I want to talk to you about something. Do you have a minute?"

She glanced over toward the Starbucks. Claire was watching them, and she gave Ember a thumbs-up sign. Oh, jeez. Claire had such a wrong idea about her and Charles. And if they slipped away even for a few seconds, it would only encourage her. Still, she was curious to know what he wanted. "Sure. What's up?"

Charles paid for her gum and his candy and led her to the produce aisle. He leaned against an apple bin. "I need some help with my story."

"Your story?" So this was about work. Ember felt a mixture of disappointment and annoyance—disappointment that he wanted to talk about work and annoyance at herself for feeling that way. They were in the Co-worker Zone. That was how it should be, and she was lucky it wasn't more complicated than that.

Charles lowered his voice. "Yeah. The computer hacker story. I'm getting nowhere, and I need someone to do a little digging."

She picked up an apple and studied it. It felt smooth and solid, but a brown spot near the stem marred its shiny red surface. Eventually the whole thing would be rotten.

"So what do you think?" Charles asked. "Can you help me?"

Ember shook her head. Digging was the last thing she wanted to do. "Sorry. Not happening."

"What? Why not? You're perfect for this."

"Me? Why?"

"Because you hardly have any friends."

Ember dropped the apple back into the bin. "Gee, thanks." She started to walk away, but Charles blocked her way.

"No, wait. That came out wrong. Very wrong. I just meant … you're still new here, so it's not like everyone already knows everything about you … and your family, and your family's family." He sighed. "When I ask people questions, it comes off as weird. Like I'm prying and suspicious. With you, it'll seem more normal."

Ember frowned. She'd avoided asking questions since she'd arrived in Boyd County because she didn't want people prying into *her* life. She saw no reason to start now. "Sorry. I'm a photographer, not an investigative reporter."

"Right." Charles stepped aside, and Ember headed back toward the Starbucks. He called after her. "You know, sometimes I think you hide behind your camera."

Ember stopped. She turned and glared. What was that supposed to mean? True, she did feel safer behind the camera. When she peered through the viewfinder, it became her world, blocking everything else out. Best of all, she was never in the shot. She could disappear. Still, Charles had no right to say that. He didn't know anything about her. She walked back up to him. "What makes you think I want to hide?"

Charles met her gaze. "Oh, maybe … *everything*. It's like you've wrapped this huge veil of secrecy around yourself. Anytime anyone asks the simplest question, you change the subject. Do you realize I don't even know the name of a single friend of yours from back in Philadelphia? I don't even know your boyfriend's name—that guy from the photo. Assuming he's your boyfriend. Or was." He threw his hands up in the air. "Hell, I don't even know if you *have* a boyfriend."

"Would it matter?"

Charles shook his head. "There you go again, avoiding the subject, answering questions with questions. Why can't you just tell me? Do you or do you not have a boyfriend?"

"Fine. Yes, I have a boyfriend. At least I did. I still might, but things are … complicated. His name is Zach. He is the guy from the photo. He's a pitcher.

He's sweet and funny, and he treats me like a princess. And he's bigger than a bread box but smaller than an elephant."

The expression in Charles's eyes softened. "See. Was that so hard?"

"Now will you tell me whether it matters?"

His face grew pink. "Of course it matters. It means…"

He paused, and Ember's heart seemed to pause along with him. Please don't let him say something stupid and sappy and sentimental here in the produce aisle. She didn't think she could handle that.

"It means you're a real person, with a real past. It means you're just like everyone else after all."

Oh, crap. Tears pricked her eyes. Why did he have to say that? How she wished it were true. She heard a burst of laughter from the direction of the Starbucks, and she looked over at the table full of her friends all joking and giggling and cheerfully sipping their coffees. If only she could be like that.

"What's the matter?" He put his hand on her arm. "Is this about him—Zach? Because I wouldn't have brought it up if I'd realized it was such a sore—"

"Tell you what." Ember shrugged off his hand and blinked away her tears. "You stop talking about this, and I'll help you with your story."

Charles nodded. "Of course. I'm sorry. Listen, you

don't have to—"

"I'm in." She took a deep breath. She was Ember O'Malley now—a smart, sweet, talented girl from Philly with nothing to hide and no shameful GIFs to haunt her every waking hour. Maybe if she started acting as though that were reality, it would become reality, at least for the next couple of weeks. "Tell me who you need me to talk to, and I'll talk to them."

# CHAPTER THIRTY

"**Y**ou're a fake and a phony, and I wish I'd never laid eyes on you!" Claire burst into tears, turned, and ran.

Ember smiled. She was good. Really good. And the way Ryan gazed at her—either he was a heck of an actor as well, or he was into her. They made an adorable Sandy Olsson and Danny Zuko. She zoomed in on Ryan's face and captured his wistful puppy dog eyes. Maybe Claire would finally admit he liked her when she saw this.

She removed her flash and packed up her camera case. This had been fun, though not very productive. Ember had convinced Charles that the only way she could meet people and ask questions was if he let her shoot more than football games, so he'd assigned her to just about every activity in school this week—the 4-H Club rally, the debate team competition, the math club meeting, and now the *Grease* rehearsal.

None of it was getting her anywhere. It reminded her of surfing—she couldn't even get up on the board. Once she found out someone's name and grade and what they liked most about whatever activity she happened to be shooting, what else could she ask? *By the way, how much do you know about computers, and would you have any reason to want to hack the school's system?* It didn't exactly come up in normal conversation.

Not that she was complaining. It felt great to take photos of something besides a bunch of guys running around in helmets and pads. Like that picture of Ryan—she could actually capture people's expressions for a change. Plus, she had a feeling that seeing the assignment board with her name all over it Monday had made Marissa nervous. So that was kind of fun.

Ember noticed a girl sitting on the floor at the side of the stage, leaning against the cutout of Greased Lightning and studying her script. She walked over. Might as well give it a try.

The girl glanced up as she approached. She had

dark frizzy hair pulled back with a huge butterfly clip and wore the brightest pink lipstick Ember had ever seen.

"Hi. I'm Ember, from the *Bulletin*. Sorry to interrupt, but—"

"I'm Sarah, a.k.a. Rizzo." She waved her script.

"Rizzo? Great part."

Sarah sighed. "I guess. But it's also hard. She's so… different from me."

Ember nodded and sat down next to her. "Well, that's probably a good thing."

"You mean that I'm not a bitch? And a slut? And possibly pregnant?"

Ember winced. "Well … yeah."

Sarah pointed to the page she'd been studying. "Thing is, there's a lot more to her than that. If she was all bitch, I could go to town with it. But she's not. She's also … a girl. Like us."

Ember nodded. "It's been a while since I saw the movie, but I remember feeling bad for her. She seemed… misunderstood."

"Yes! Misunderstood. Did you know Rizzo is actually her last name? Guess her first name."

Ember shook her head. "No idea."

"Betty. Isn't that awesome? Betty! In this scene where she and Kenickie are making out, she asks him to call her that. It's like she doesn't want to be 'Rizzo' with him."

Ember got that. Holy wow, did she get it. Though "Rizzo" was better than "Slutkowski" any day. "So you need to play both. Betty and Rizzo."

"Right, and that's what's kicking my butt. When am I Betty, and when am I Rizzo?"

Ember cocked her head. "What do you mean? You're never going to be just one or the other. You're always both. You're Betty Rizzo."

Sarah's bright pink lips puckered, and she gazed up at the ceiling as though she was processing that. "Right. Which doesn't make it any easier."

"No, but that's one of the reasons it's such a great role."

"True." Sarah smiled and leaned in, her voice dropping to a whisper. "The other reason is that Josh Miles is Kenickie."

Josh was in Ember's phys ed class. Very cute. "Nice." She laughed and gave Sarah a fist bump. She glanced around and matched her whisper. "Hey, mind if I ask a weird question?"

"Sure."

"I realize this is kind of random, but by any chance do you know anything about the school's comp—"

"Ember!" Claire appeared at their side. "What are

you doing here? Please tell me you're taking photos. And please tell me you got one of Ryan crawling after me on his hands and knees during 'You're the One That I Want.'"

"I am, and I did." Ember pulled out her camera and scrolled through the shots. "You're going to love these. You two are beyond adorable together."

Claire rolled her eyes. "How many times do I have to tell you? We're not together."

"Could have fooled me," Sarah said.

"I know, right?" Ember tilted her viewfinder to face Sarah. "Check out this last shot—the way he's looking at her."

"Oh, stop." Claire put her hand over the screen. "It's called acting. Ryan and I have been friends since the second grade. Dating him would be like dating my brother."

"Well, you're the one who told me Boyd County is incestuous."

"Ew!" Claire laughed. "It's a figure of speech."

Ember shrugged and leaned in. "Then it's a good thing he's not your brother. You know he's not. In fact, I think you're exceedingly aware of it."

Claire blushed and turned away. "You're crazy." She grabbed Sarah. "Come on, Ms. Davis wants us to run through 'Summer Nights' again."

Ember waved goodbye to them and slipped out the theater's side door. She hadn't asked Sarah, or anyone for that matter, about the computer system, but whatever. None of them seemed like the criminal type. As she made her way down the hall, she heard footsteps approaching from behind.

"Yo, Emily."

She wheeled around to find Tommy striding toward her. Speaking of the criminal type. "Don't call me that," she whispered. "What is wrong with you? And what are you doing here?"

"I run tech crew. Your flash was messing up my lighting."

"Yeah, well, it was just rehearsal. You don't have to worry about me using it on show night. What do you want?"

"You seem to be getting around this week. I mean, not the way you *used* to get around, but … " He raised his eyebrows and gave her a creepy grin.

"Screw you. What are you, a stalker? What do you care what I'm doing?"

"Oh, I don't care. You can hang out with the Debate Team all week long if you want."

Right. Because they weren't likely to be juicing up on steroids. "So what is it? Maybe you want me to set up a shoot with the tech crew? Feeling left out?"

"Hardly. Tech enjoys the shadows. We don't need the spotlight like those narcissists in there."

Ember narrowed her eyes and glared. "Well, I know *you* enjoy the shadows, Mr. Meet Me Under the Bleachers."

Tommy took a step toward her and grabbed her wrist. His face was just inches from hers, and his breath stunk of garlic and milk. "Watch yourself. You don't want to go there, Miss Slut-kow-ski." He spat out the name, each syllable a bullet piercing her armor of anonymity.

It was the first time in more than a month she'd heard that name. Ember blanched. The stench of Tommy's breath and the sting of his words made her head swim. She pulled away, turned and ran. She had to get away. Away from him. Away from whatever he knew about her.

# CHAPTER THIRTY-ONE

Ember clipped on her mermaid ear cuff. She loved how it looked with her new hair. Maybe tonight would be the night she could wear it—a little piece of the shore out here in farmland. She finished getting dressed just as the doorbell rang—Claire, picking her up for a party. She glanced in the mirror one last time. She wasn't sure what kids wore to parties around here, but she assumed jeans and the blue-and-white striped sweater would work. She realized this was the first time she'd looked forward to a party since that night at Molly's.

She ripped off the ear cuff. Tonight was not the night.

"Eleven," her mom called as she headed out the door.

"Midnight?"

"Eleven. Sharp."

Ember sighed. "Fine." At least she hadn't insisted on driving her and meeting the kid's parents, though she had called earlier to make sure they knew about the party. Mortifying.

Ember played with the radio in Claire's Ford Focus. "So, do you think this will just be the kids from *Grease*, or will other people show up too?"

"Other people? Hoping for anyone in particular?"

Ember settled on a Keith Urban song—the radio here seemed to be all country, all the time—and turned to look out the window. "No. Just … other people."

"Because the people from *Grease* aren't good enough for you?"

"No, I don't mean that." Ember turned back and put her hand on Claire's arm. "You know I don't mean that, right? You all seem great."

Claire nodded. "Right. Well, to answer your question, I think it's possible Charles could show up."

Ember's face grew warm. "I didn't mention Charles."

"Didn't have to. My middle name is 'Voyant,' you know."

"What? Oh, very funny." Ember couldn't help but giggle. "Well, you're wrong about Charles. It's not like that with us. Now, with you and Ryan … "

Now it was Claire's turn to blush. "So what's the deal with your phone?"

She was changing the subject, but Ember gladly let her. "Apparently my replacement got lost in the mail, but the new one is supposed to arrive tomorrow."

It was taking the Marshals Service longer to give it back than Deputy Steuben had promised—whether because they were slow or because he'd lied in the first place about it taking just a few days she wasn't sure. Of course, getting it back wouldn't change anything. She couldn't contact Zach anymore. Little Emmie Oakley was gone—wiped off the face of the Internet, never to DM again—and Steuben would make sure she couldn't set up another account. Ember would have to wait until the trial to see Zach and find out whether they were still together.

Three weeks. It felt like forever.

\*\*\*

They arrived at the party to find the "Beauty School

Dropout" scene being reenacted in the living room, except the guy playing the Frankie Avalon part kept mashing it up with random Jason Derulo lyrics.

When he saw Claire and Ember, he rushed over, danced between them, and put his arms around their waists. "*Talk dirty to me.*"

Ember pulled away. For a moment, she felt that old sense of panic and nausea, but Claire's laughter snapped her out of it. He was playing around. It was a joke, nothing more, and all those kids howling and pointing were laughing *with* her, not *at* her. She smiled and even pumped her fist a few times as the guy dragged her and Claire up the stairs with him, "to that malt shop in the sky."

As the song ended, everyone burst into applause.

Ember turned to Claire and laughed. "Why do I feel like I've stepped onto the set of *Glee*?"

Claire shook her head. "I have no idea what just happened here. We're not always like this, I swear."

They made their way to the kitchen and poured themselves some punch. No alcohol. Ember suspected a couple of the kids may have spiked their drinks with their own stash, but still, it was a lot tamer than the parties back home. At least, the ones she'd gone to.

"Hey, Claire. Hey, Ember."

She turned to find Ryan gazing at her friend with

that same expression he'd had in the photo. "Hello, Ryan." Ember nudged Claire. "You know what? I need to find the bathroom." She slipped away and headed toward the back door. The place supposedly had a serious party deck, and she was curious to see who was out there. Not that she had anyone specific in mind.

The deck was packed with kids from different grades and different groups and possibly different schools. She pushed her way through the crowd to the far side, where it overlooked a huge expanse of some unidentifiable former crop.

"A lot different from back home, I'll bet."

She turned to find Charles standing behind her. He wore a loose white tee with a flannel shirt over it. Somehow it totally worked on him. She smiled. "Yeah. A lot different."

"Do you miss it?"

She nodded. She wished she could tell him about it—the moon's gentle glow on the water, the roar of the surf, the ocean breeze. Tears pricked the corners of her eyes.

He stepped up beside her and leaned against the rail. "Come on, now. It can't be all bad. It's quieter here, right? There's less traffic. And the air's cleaner."

She glanced away. "It takes some getting used to." That much was true.

As the crowd pressed in against them, Charles's forearm brushed up against hers. Even through her thick sweater, she could feel the heat from his body, and she gripped the rail to steady herself. Why did he have such an effect on her?

He leaned in closer. He smelled like fresh hay and hard work, and when she looked into his eyes, they drew her in like a riptide—sudden and fierce and inescapable. Her mother's warning to her as a child played like a recording in her head: *If you ever get caught in a riptide, don't fight it. Go with the flow until it releases you.* Her heart raced.

"So," he whispered. "Any luck?"

"Luck?"

"With the story. Did you find any leads?"

Aaand … the riptide released her. This was about work. As usual. She tore her eyes away from his. "Not exactly. I told you, I'm not an investigative reporter."

Charles frowned. "The school changed its security settings last week, and already the system's been hacked again. Whoever is responsible knows what he—or she—is doing. You're sure you didn't see or hear anything suspicious?"

She shrugged. "Well, I found it suspicious that practically every member of the debate team wanted to be on the 'pro' side of the GMO debate. What's that about? Shouldn't it be the other way around?"

Charles laughed and shook his head. "Ember, Ember. Such a city girl. You have a lot to learn."

Before she could protest that maybe he and his country friends had a lot to learn, someone bumped her from behind, slamming her into Charles and causing him to spill half his soda over the side of the railing. "Sorry! I—"

"Not your fault. Come on, let's get out of here." Charles motioned for her to follow him and headed for the staircase at the side of the deck. He led her across the yard toward a bench behind an old shed, where he sat down and stretched out his long legs. "That's not really my scene," he said. "As I mentioned, I prefer quiet, less traffic."

Ember eased down next to him. They sat for a while in silence, but it wasn't an uncomfortable silence. It was nice. Easy.

Finally, Charles spoke. "So. I know you don't like to talk about where you're from. Want to tell me where you're going?"

"Where I'm going?"

"Yeah. Or where you want to go. Your hopes and dreams and all that."

Ember blinked. No one had ever asked her that before—certainly no boy. "Well, I want to go to college.

I'm thinking Long Island U, because they have a really good photography program."

"Cool. Then what?"

She shrugged. "Become a photographer, I guess."

"What kind?"

"I don't know. The kind that makes lots of money."

Charles leaned toward her. "Come on, tell me. What kind of photographer do you want to be?"

Ember pulled the sleeves of her sweater down over her hands. She drew up her knees and hugged them into her chest. She'd never talked about this to anyone. What if it sounded stupid? "I want to be a portrait photographer, but not the kind that takes pictures in the studio; the kind that takes pictures of people out in the real world, being who they are and doing the things they love to do." She glanced at him. He didn't look as though he thought she was stupid. He looked... interested. "You know how they say a picture is worth a thousand words? Well, I want to tell stories about people. True stories. Stories of who they are deep down." Like that picture of Trina. The one that proved she wasn't too old or too cool to love the thrill of the wind tugging a kite up, up, up into the sky. "I want to take pictures that push past people's images and uncovers something real."

Charles whistled. "Now *that's* a dream."

"Sorry. It's silly, right?"

"No, not at all." Charles leaned in even closer, his face just a few inches from hers. His voice was barely a whisper. "I didn't mean it's an impossible dream. I meant it's the kind of dream worth dreaming."

Ember's face grew warm. Thankfully, it was too dark for him to see her blushing. For a moment, she thought he might kiss her, but then he pulled away. He bent over, plucked a long strand of grass growing at the foot of the bench, and began chewing on it. "So what else? Where do you want to live?"

Ember tilted her head back and gazed up at the stars. There were so many here. "I'd love to live somewhere near the water." She hesitated, choosing her words carefully. "Every summer, my mom used to take us to the Jersey Shore for vacation. I loved the feel of the sand under my feet, the sound of the waves, the way the sky and the sea melted into each other on the horizon." She closed her eyes and allowed herself to imagine it. A breeze struck up, and she shivered.

"Here, take this." Charles took off his flannel shirt and draped it around her shoulders.

"Thanks, but you'll freeze in that T-shirt. I'm fine." She tried to give it back, but he refused. She had to admit, it felt nice. Warm and soft and kind. "What about you? You said you wanted to be a journalist?"

"Yeah. I want to tell stories too. Only … less efficiently, I guess. I love words." He sighed. "Unfortunately, that probably *is* an impossible dream. My family has owned our ranch for more than a hundred years. They need me to take it over."

"Doesn't seem like such a bad life."

"It's not. I don't hate it. Doesn't exactly feed the creative spirit, though."

They sat for a while talking about little things and big things, occasionally falling silent. Ember couldn't remember the last time she'd felt so relaxed. Maybe because she couldn't remember the last time she'd been herself. It was weird. She was being Ember, but she felt more real than she had in a very long time. She leaned back into the bench and shut her eyes.

What seemed like moments later, a crashing sound from the direction of the deck startled her. Somehow she was leaning up against Charles's shoulder.

"Oh my gosh, did I fall asleep?"

He grinned. "Maybe."

"That's embarrassing. What time is it?" She reached for her nonexistent phone.

Charles pulled his out of his front shirt pocket. "Ten after eleven."

"What?" Ember jumped up. "Oh, man. I am so dead. I was supposed to be home by eleven." She rushed toward the house with Charles behind her. As she squeezed through the now even larger crowd on the deck, she heard someone call her name. She turned to find the girl from the musical, Sarah, waving frantically.

"Ember! Claire's been looking all over for you. You'd better let her know you're okay."

Ember made it across the deck and into the kitchen, where she found Claire on her phone.

Claire ran over and hugged her. "She's here," she said to the person on the other end. "I'm so sorry, Mrs. O'Malley. I didn't mean to worry you. We're going to head out—what? You just pulled up, as in, pulled up here, at the party?" Claire widened her eyes at Ember.

"Oh, man. This is not good." Ember wound through the crowd toward the living room. Maybe she could get out the door and into the car before her mom could make a scene. She turned and waved goodbye to Charles, and as she turned back around, she saw something that made her even more nervous than the thought of her mom bursting into the party.

There, at the front door, stood Marissa talking to Tricia.

# CHAPTER THIRTY-TWO

*Eleven weeks earlier*

"She's my little sister. I'm allowed to be hysterical." Emily's eyes filled with tears. How could Zach insist she was overreacting? What part of "bullet hole" did he not understand?

"Calm down." He laid his hands on her shoulders. "I'm telling you, if you'll just let it—"

"No! I won't let it go." She pulled away, strode out of the coffee shop, and headed toward the pier. Part of her wanted to be alone, but part hoped he'd follow her. They'd never argued before the night of the bonfire. Now, for the past few days, it seemed all they did was fight. The wind whipped her hair into her face as she walked out to the end of the pier. The air had a bite to it that she hadn't felt in months. Summer was beginning to give way to autumn's chill.

She leaned over the railing at the end of the pier and closed her eyes as the sea spray mixed with the tears on her cheeks. How had everything gotten so complicated, so frightening, so quickly?

She felt him behind her before he even spoke.

"I'm sorry, babe." He pulled her away from the railing and drew her into his chest. "I'm trying to protect you from getting hurt. You know that, right?"

She nodded, though she was crying even harder now.

He buried his face in her hair, his lips against her ear. "I wasn't going to say anything, but I talked to Jimmy about this whole thing."

She pulled away. "You what? When?"

"Shh. It's okay." Zach led her to a nearby bench and sat down, pulling her onto his lap. "I called him last night, after you told me about the picture."

"You shouldn't have done that."

"I know, but I had to find out what was going on."

"What did he say?"

Zach looked away. "You know Jimmy. He talks big. Half the time you don't know what to believe. But one thing he said, I do believe. He said this all goes away if you tell the cops to forget about it. Tell them you made it up, or were confused, or whatever."

Emily bit her lip. She wanted to scream, but instead, she said nothing. A girl was dead, and Jimmy's blue beer concoction was to blame. She didn't make it up. She wasn't confused. And she would not, could not tell the cops to "forget it." For the second time that afternoon, she walked away from Zach. This time she didn't want him to follow her, not even a little bit. This time she was afraid of what she might say to him if he did.

What she didn't know was that it would be the last time she'd see him for three months.

When she walked in the front door, two deputies sat waiting in her living room. They gave her fifteen minutes to pack a suitcase before they whisked her, her mom, and her sister away.

# CHAPTER THIRTY-THREE

Thanksgiving started out quiet. Ember was grounded after the Saturday night debacle, but it didn't matter much. All of her friends had family stuff going on. She and Tricia helped their mom cook a small turkey with dressing and sweet potatoes and parsley and a whole table full of fixings, but somehow it felt all wrong. She missed their kitchen back in Jersey, with its temperamental oven, and stained linoleum floor, and the faucet that leaked unless you turned the handle to its precise "off" position.

"How about we start a new tradition this year?" her mom asked as they finished eating. "In our new life as the O'Malleys, the mom takes a nap after dinner while the daughters clean up."

"That's a horrible idea," Ember said. "Besides, we're not going to be O'Malleys much longer. You can't call something a tradition if it only happens once."

"I'll clean up." Tricia grabbed a couple of plates and took them to the sink. "Who knows? We might still be O'Malleys next year."

Ember sighed at the hopeful tone in her sister's voice. "Don't count on it." She grabbed the bowl of leftover cranberries and wrapped plastic over it. "We'll be back in Jersey by Christmas if everything goes as planned."

Everything *would* go as planned. At least, she hoped it would. Didn't she?

Halfway through washing the pots and pans, they were startled by the sound of the doorbell. She and Tricia looked at each other. They'd never had a visitor here before. Well, except for Deputy Steuben, but surely he wasn't working on Thanksgiving.

"Quiet," their mother warned. She crept over to the window and peered out through a crack in the curtain. She turned and smiled. "It's your friend. The editor boy."

Ember's eyes grew wide. Not the editor boy. She was a mess. She had on ratty sweatpants, no makeup, and … was that a gravy stain on her shirt? Oh, jeez. She motioned for her mother to wait, but it was too late. She was already opening the door and inviting Charles in for pumpkin pie. Lovely.

"Hey, Charles." Ember draped her right hand over her left shoulder in hopes of covering up the gravy stain. "What are you doing here?"

Charles's smile disappeared. "I wanted to wish you a happy Thanksgiving. Sorry. I guess I should have called first?"

"No, no." Ember shook her head. She was being rude. "I'm glad you came."

She *was* glad he came. And that he was thinking about her. She'd been thinking about him this week, too. More than she cared to admit. More than she'd thought about Zach.

Charles glanced back and forth between her and her sister, taking in the dishtowel Tricia was holding. He pointed toward the kitchen. "How about you wash, I dry … " He pointed to Tricia. "And you put away?"

Tricia nodded and handed over her towel, her eyes shining. Ember glanced at her mom and suppressed a smile. He was quite the charmer.

After dishes and her mom's homemade pumpkin pie, Charles stood and stretched. "Thank you, Mrs. O'Malley. That was amazing." He glanced at Ember.

"Would it be okay if I take your daughter for a quick walk?"

To Ember's surprise, her mom nodded. "Don't be too long."

He really was a charmer. Ember rushed to put on a jacket before her mother could change her mind.

The streets were empty—even emptier than usual, and warm lights glowed in the windows of every house. The blue glow of televisions flickered here and there as families gathered to watch Thanksgiving football.

"I'm sorry about the other night," Charles said. "I should have woken you up. I had no idea Claire was looking for you."

"Don't apologize. You had no way of knowing my ridiculously early curfew." Ember glanced up at him shyly. "Anyway, it was kind of worth it."

True, she'd slept through it, but just knowing she'd been pressed up against Charles in his sexy white T-shirt for almost an hour had caused butterflies to take flight in her stomach on more than a few occasions over the past week.

Charles smiled into the distance. "Did you know that you talk in your sleep?"

Ember stopped. What had she said? She tried to keep her voice even. "I do not."

"You do." He turned to face her. "It's a little freaky,

I have to tell you."

She shrugged, still attempting to appear nonchalant. "What did I say?"

"Nothing that made any sense. Something about blue beer and purple kites. Dreams are bizarre, aren't they?"

Ember turned and started walking again. She didn't trust her expression. "My dreams never make any sense. They're obviously colorful, though."

They walked in silence for a while, until Charles cleared his throat. "So. I've been wondering about something."

"Okay."

"Remember in the Super Saver, when you were talking about that guy from Philly, and you said things were complicated. What does complicated mean, exactly?"

Ember stopped again. What *did* "complicated" mean at this point? She wasn't sure she even knew. She and Zach hadn't communicated in two weeks, and she had no way to reach him. For some reason, all of his Internet accounts had gone completely silent, so she had no idea what he was up to. The last thing she knew, surfgurrl had called him her boyfriend.

Meanwhile, here in front of her was a boy who, despite all of her efforts to convince herself otherwise, she was clearly crushing on. A nerdy, strip-dancing, football-superhero, pirate-loving cowboy who thought her dreams were worth dreaming and who stopped by out of the blue to wish her a happy Thanksgiving.

Of course, he also thought her name was Ember O'Malley and that she was a nice girl from Philly.

Ember turned and headed back toward home. She chose her words carefully. "When people say 'complicated,' it's because they don't want to have to explain. Or because they can't." Her voice caught. "I'm sorry, Charles. I wish I could give you a better answer."

Charles said nothing until they reached her front yard. "You okay?"

Ember nodded, tears pricking the corners of her eyes. "I'm good. And I do appreciate your coming over today. And helping with the dishes. That was super nice."

He shrugged. "I'm a nice guy. And simple. As in, not complicated."

Ember couldn't help but smile. "And I like that about you."

# CHAPTER THIRTY-FOUR

The next Monday, after football and cheer practice ended, Ember met up with a bunch of kids to go to the bridge. Ever since she'd moved to Boyd County, she'd heard people talk about an old covered bridge where teenagers drank and partied and generally got into mischief, but she'd never been there, and she was a little nervous about going now. She was still grounded, but she'd lied and told her mom she had a photo assignment for the *Bulletin*.

She wanted to see what the place was like, and she wanted to feel a part of something, a part of a group. And, yes, she wanted any excuse to hang out with Charles again. She would be heading back to Jersey in about a week. If things worked out, she might never see him again.

"Wine cooler, beer, or water?" He fished a bottle of each out of an ice bucket as she walked up.

Ember took the water and smiled. "Thanks." She peered up at the bridge, its wood faded to a pale gray, its roof falling apart at the far end. It spanned a smallish creek, though the size of the banks indicated it had once been much larger and deeper. "So this is the infamous bridge." She tried unsuccessfully to keep the disappointment out of her voice. What had she expected? It was like so many other things here. Old. Bland. Washed out.

"Yep. Lots of water has gone under that baby."

Ember groaned. "You are so lame."

Charles grinned and motioned for her to follow him through the growing crowd and up onto the creaky wooden planks. He stopped just inside the entrance and peered around. "In all seriousness, if this bridge could talk, it would have some crazy stories to tell."

The light was dimmer and softer in here, and the smell of moss and pine permeated the air. Ember traced her finger along the etchings in the bridge walls.

*JS + BD 4EVER.*

*Britt Luvs T-Bro.*

*MD <3 OT.*

She was suddenly very aware that she and Charles were alone, and that many, many couples had been alone in here before them. Not that they were a couple.

He led her to the center of the span, where a hole in the wall looked out onto a small waterfall below. A mottled brown bird with a bright yellow chest sat atop a post on the far bank.

"Look how pretty." Too bad she didn't have her camera. She'd left it in the car because … well, she knew as well as anyone that cameras and partying didn't mix.

"That's a meadowlark." Charles leaned in close and whispered. "If we're lucky, he'll sing for us."

They stood still and listened for several minutes until at last the bird craned its neck and warbled a sweet, happy tune.

"Wow." Ember had never heard anything like it. She was used to the screech of seagulls and the short pips of sandpipers.

"Pretty cool, isn't it?" Charles took out his phone and began scrolling. "I helped rescue a baby meadowlark last spring."

"Really?"

"Yep. A cat had killed his mom and the rest of the nestlings. They build their nests on the ground, so that happens a lot." Charles stopped at a photo of the bird and showed her. "This little guy was running around chirping up a storm. I brought him inside and raised him for a few days before we could get him to the rescue."

"Oh my gosh. He's adorable."

"That's what I thought, until he turned out to be a total pain in the butt. Had to feed him constantly. I spent hours digging up bugs and picking berries, and after all that, it turned out his favorite food was Frosted Flakes."

Ember laughed. "How funny. And sweet."

Charles fumbled with his phone as he tucked it back into his pocket. When he spoke again, his voice had a rough, grainy quality to it. "*You're* sweet."

"Me?" Guys had called her a lot of things lately, but sweet wasn't one of them.

"Yes. And pretty, and smart, and talented, and …" He leaned toward her, and she closed her eyes so he could kiss her. It was a warm, tender kiss, nothing like the kiss in the barn. Where that kiss had been a tidal wave, rough and disorienting, this one was a gentle whirlpool that sent her stomach, her head, her heart a-twirl. And where she had felt immediate regret after the first kiss, she knew that no matter what happened, no matter how things turned out, she would never regret this.

"Sorry," Charles whispered. "That was … not simple."

"Oh, but it was," she said.

"I'm really glad you came. I'm glad you're here."

Ember rested her forehead against his chest. He felt sturdy and safe. "Me too. But I'm dead if my mom finds out."

Charles laughed. "I didn't mean here, to the bridge. Though I'm glad about that too. I meant I'm glad you came to Boyd County. I'm glad you came into the *Bulletin* office that day with your old-school portfolio and your adorable smile and those weird little tan lines on your ear. Which, by the way, have almost faded."

Ember pulled away and looked up at him. "You noticed the tan lines?"

He raised one eyebrow. "I noticed everything about you. I didn't understand most of it. Still don't. But I notice. And I'm really, really, glad you're here. I almost can't remember what it was like before you came."

She leaned back into him. Oh, my. He was into her. A part of her wanted to accept that, own it, but the truth was, he didn't understand. He didn't understand any of it, and if he did, he wouldn't be so glad she came. She pressed her face into his shirt so he couldn't see her tears. Why couldn't things be simple? She was a teenage girl standing in the middle of an abandoned bridge in the arms of a boy whose kisses made her want to forget the rest of the world existed. Why couldn't that be the whole story?

She stood like that for a while, melting into his breathing and the steady beat of his heart, until a shout and a splash drew her attention to the water below.

A guy from the football team had jumped in, fully clothed. Two other guys stood on the bank laughing at him.

Charles leaned out. "Schmidt, you idiot. What are you doing?"

"It was a dare. These losers thought I wouldn't do it."

"You mean those losers standing over there, all nice and dry and warm?" He lowered his voice and murmured into Ember's ear. "Schmidt's not exactly the sharpest tool in the shed."

"Who's that up there with you?" Schmidt stood and waded closer, stumbling across the rocks on the creek bed. "Oh, ho! It's the new girl." He turned and called to his teammates. "Hey, guys, Charles has a girlfriend. It's that photographer chick."

"Shut up," Charles shouted. "Her name is Ember. And you've had a few too many. Get out and dry off."

Schmidt stopped and peered up at them, his face suddenly thoughtful. "Look at you two love birds.

Kind of like Romeo and Juliet up there on the balcony. Wherefore art thou and all that. Whatever you do, don't jump."

Ember looked at Charles. "Jump? Why would we jump?"

Charles shook his head and shrugged.

"You know. The balcony scene in *Romeo and Juliet*." Schmidt threw his hands up in the air. "Everyone says it's such a tragedy, but I say it's stupid. They fall in love and kill themselves."

Ember gave him an incredulous stare. "By jumping."

"Yeah. Suicide."

Ember and Charles burst out laughing.

"Of course. The famous balcony scene," Charles said.

"One. Two. Three. Jump!" Ember added.

Schmidt looked back and forth at them, his face growing bright red. Finally, he turned to his teammates on the bank, who were falling over themselves in hysterics. "What the … why would you do that?"

"Maybe you should've read it like you were supposed to," one of them yelled back.

"I mean, come on, Schmidt," said the other. "You seriously believed Mercutio was a droid?"

Schmidt smacked his hand on the water. "Screw you guys."

Ember clutched Charles's arm. "A droid! Something tells me he didn't do too well on that test."

Charles snorted. "Like I said, he was never too bright. He once wrote an entire essay about Dickens's *A Christmas Carol* ... all about a guy named George Bailey whose bank was about to go under until his guardian angel helped save the day."

"You're kidding."

"I swear."

"How the heck can he—" Ember stopped as a thought struck her. Oh, no. How could she have missed it? She leaned against the side of the bridge, her knees suddenly weak. Of course. It made so much sense.

"Are you okay?" Charles's expression registered somewhere between concern and alarm. "You look like you're about to puke."

Ember shook her head and bolted off the bridge. She needed time alone to think. She finally understood what Tommy Walker and the coach were doing that day under the bleachers.

The question was, what should she do about it?

# CHAPTER THIRTY-FIVE

"**G**ive me a B!"

Ember slouched over on the bleachers and cradled her head in her hands. Would this pep rally never end?

For the past two days, she'd debated. Should she nark out Tommy Walker, Coach Sebastian, Schmidt, and whichever other players might be fixing their grades, or should she keep her mouth shut?

No doubt everyone here would hate her if she ruined the school's chance to go to the state championship game. And ultimately, that's all it was—a game. It wasn't as though someone had drowned. On the other hand, she knew that somewhere out there was a team who deserved to play on Saturday, a legit team. They were not having a pep rally. They would not be on TV and in the papers. And they would not be adding a trophy to their school's trophy case. Not to mention there were kids here, like Claire, studying their butts off to get grades they'd actually earned. It was so unfair.

Of course, if she ratted out Tommy, he would reveal her secrets to the entire school. Part of her was terrified of that prospect, but another part thought it might be for the best. She was going back to Jersey in a few days anyway. Maybe it was time for everyone here to see the real her. She could leave without a bunch of loose ends and false hopes. Charles, Claire, and everyone else would realize she was a phony. If she never came back, they'd know why. And they'd have no reason to miss her.

After the rally, she weaved her way through the sea of red and white to the nearest bathroom. All that misplaced school spirit nauseated her. She walked in to find Claire at one of the sinks, freshening her makeup.

"Hey, Ember! Wasn't that fun? So much energy from the crowd." She wiped at her mascara. "Of course, now I'm a sweaty mess."

Ember forced a smile. "Yeah. Great job." She walked over and stood next to her, checking out their reflections in the mirror. She recalled that first day they'd met, when Claire had sat down and talked to her before first-period history, and invited her to sit with the cheer squad at lunch, and asked her to go to the game that night, and even visited her in the hospital afterward, stuffed teddy and cell number in hand. Ember had thought she didn't want any friends, didn't need them, but somehow Claire changed all that in a single day.

"Are you okay?" Claire put her arm around Ember's shoulder and squeezed. "You look sad."

"I'm fine. I just … " Ember sighed. "Can I ask you something?"

"Anything."

"What would you do if you could have a do-over?"

"A do-over? Of what?"

"Everything. What if you could change your whole life, your whole identity? What would you change?"

Claire shrugged and screwed up her lips. "I don't know. Nothing." She paused. "Except maybe I'd be braver. I'd tell Ryan I thought he was hot."

Ember laughed. Claire was so … real. She wouldn't want her to change a thing. Though it *was* about time she admitted Ryan was hot. Ember gave Claire a hug, and suddenly she found herself crying. Maybe it was because she knew she'd miss Claire, or maybe it was because she'd miss Charles even more. Charles. He'd been avoiding her the past few days. Not that she could blame him. She had a way of kissing him and running away, and she supposed that might put a guy off.

Most likely, though, she was crying because she wished her do-over could last forever—that she could take Ember back to New Jersey and be a normal teenage girl, known as "Red" or "Photographer Chick" or anything at all besides "Slutkowski."

"Ember, are you crying?" Claire patted her gently on the back. "What's wrong? Tell me."

Ember's silent tears turned to sobs, and she pulled away. She wanted to tell Claire what was wrong. She wanted to tell her everything. She couldn't do that, of course, but she could tell her about Tommy Walker. Maybe that would help. Get it off her chest, make her feel better.

She grabbed a handful of tissues, blew her nose, and dried her eyes. "I do have something I need to tell you. But I don't think you're going to like it."

# CHAPTER THIRTY-SIX

Ember pulled up the hood of her coat. A light drizzle cast a gray pall over the field. Her stomach rolled like waves in a storm. Was she really going to do this?

Claire had convinced her it was the best way: confront Coach Sebastian and Schmidt, and let them turn themselves in. To her relief, Claire hadn't been angry or upset when she'd told her about the hacking scheme. In fact, she had encouraged her to speak up even though it would surely mean forfeiting their trip to the state championships. Claire, the consummate cheerleader.

Coach stood on the sidelines while his players executed drills on the field. Ember sidled up to him, glad now for the hood. It allowed her some anonymity.

Maybe she could say her piece and get out of there without causing a scene. She scanned the field for Charles and spotted him off in the far end zone. Yes, this could work out okay after all.

"Mr. Sebastian." She tried to sound confident, authoritative. "I need to talk to you. You and Marcus Schmidt."

He gave her a dismissive look up and down. He seemed not to recognize her. "I'm a little busy here."

"It's important."

"As important as state? I'm guessing not." He swiveled back around and shouted at one of the players. "Come on, Wilkes! You gotta be quicker off the ball than that!"

"It's about Schmidt's grades."

That got Coach's attention. His head snapped around, and he practically snarled at her, but then he seemed to catch himself, and his curled lip morphed into a half smile. "Grades are confidential. Afraid I can't help you there." Again he turned his back to her.

Her phone buzzed.

Claire: Tommy is on the way.

Across the field, Claire was doing stretches by the bleachers with the cheer squad. She waved and gave Ember a thumbs-up.

Ember groaned. She had asked her not to involve

Tommy, had said that once Coach and Schmidt turned themselves in, he would no doubt be implicated. But Claire insisted it would be better to confront them all at once and offered to have one of her friends on tech crew send him down to the field. Awesome. So much for not creating a scene.

"Listen, Coach. We can do this the easy way, or we can do it the hard way. Either you call Schmidt over here, or my next stop is Principal Keane's office."

Coach Sebastian turned and leaned toward her, his massive chest and shoulders dwarfing her. When he spoke, he sprayed spit onto her face. She resisted the urge to wipe it away. "Young lady, we are on the brink of winning the state football championship—something this school hasn't seen in your lifetime. Do you understand? Do you know how much it means to these players, to these kids?"

"To your career," she ventured.

He scowled and lowered his voice. "It's one grade—English—and it went from an F to a C-minus. At the rate he's going, he'll fail next semester and have to take it over anyway. You're making something out of nothing. Let it go."

Maybe he was right. After all, no one was getting hurt, not really. Except for the team that deserved to go in their place. Was it worth it to go to all this trouble for a game? Especially when it meant Tommy Walker would blow her cover?

"Okay, I'll let it go. If you bench him."

"Bench him? He's our best player. How am I supposed to explain benching him to the rest of the team? To his parents?"

Ember shrugged. "Figure it out."

"No way." Coach shook his head. "Not happening."

Ember felt her confidence deflating. She hadn't asked for this, had in fact tried to avoid getting in the middle of it. Maybe she should have followed her first instincts and stayed away.

Coach smiled, a smarmy, unctuous smile. "That's a smart girl. Now run along and … do whatever it is you teenage girls do after school these days." He turned his attention back to the players as though the matter was settled.

Ember backed up. Perhaps it was settled. As she turned to go, she glanced back toward Charles and watched him take one step, two steps, three, four, kick… and hold for the follow through. That was the most important part, he'd once told her. The follow through.

"Wimp out?" Tommy's voice startled her. "I saw the expression on your face today at the pep rally. But I knew you'd keep your mouth shut. Smart girl, *Slutkowski*."

Ember flinched. Had he really gone there? And why were he and Coach suddenly calling her a "smart girl"? She narrowed her eyes. Back in Jersey, she'd kept her mouth shut for so long, despite all the teasing and the name-calling and the groping and even the near-assault that day in the Shoot 'Em Up. She'd been "smart" and hated herself for it. In fact, one of the only things she didn't hate about her Emily Slutkowski self was that call to the police.

*Be the change you seek.*

Jaw clenched, she walked over to a megaphone lying nearby and grabbed it. If she was going to make a scene, she might as well make it spectacular. "Coach Sebastian and Marcus Schmidt. I need to speak with you. Now."

# CHAPTER THIRTY-SEVEN

Coach dropped his clipboard, the players all stopped their drills, Charles forgot to follow through, and the entire cheer squad seemed to freeze mid-jump.

Coach stormed over. "I'm warning you, don't do this. Walk away."

Ember peered past him toward Schmidt. She raised the megaphone to her lips again. "Schmidt? I'm waiting."

Slowly Schmidt, along with every other player on the team, made his way toward her. The cheerleaders bounded across the field as well. For a moment, she was transported back to that night almost three months ago, when she lay flattened, dazed, and sore with everyone staring down at her. The sense of panic she felt then was replaced now by dread. She considered some of these people her friends. That was about to change.

Ember took a deep breath and waved her hand at Tommy, Coach, and Schmidt. "I believe the three of you know what this is about. I had hoped to do this more discreetly, but apparently that's not going to happen."

Schmidt glanced nervously back and forth between Tommy and his coach. "How the … Who told her?"

"It didn't take a genius to figure it out," she said. "The question is, what are you going to do about it?"

"Do about what?" Charles looked as confused as his teammates. "Em, what's going on?"

*Em.* It was the first time he'd called her that. She shook her head. *Focus, damn it.* She explained everything, starting with the day she ran into Coach and Tommy under the bleachers and ending with the realization she'd had on the bridge.

"Are you kidding me?" asked the guy who played quarterback. He took a step toward her. "You're going to ruin our chance to go to state and play in front of every college scout in the region because this idiot doesn't know Shakespeare?"

"Dumb bitch," muttered another. "Deon should have knocked her out for good when he had the chance."

Ember searched the crowd for someone, anyone, who would stand up for her, but each face seemed angrier than the last. A few, like Deon, looked away, and even Claire seemed to shrink behind the other girls in her squad. Finally, she turned back to Charles, but his expression told her she'd get no support from him either. He wasn't angry, but he seemed … confused? Hurt? She wasn't sure. She only knew she couldn't bear to face his reaction to what was surely coming next.

She turned toward Tommy. The stage was set. Most of these people were already pissed off at her. He might as well pit the rest against her, too. But to her surprise, he said nothing, just stood there, scowling.

Finally, Claire spoke up. "You know, maybe this isn't so bad. Maybe if you guys tell the truth now—"

"Not so bad?" The quarterback interrupted her and stuck a finger in Ember's face. "This is going to be all over the news. It's going to look bad on the team, the school, all of us."

Ember's eyes flashed. "Well, maybe your coach should have thought about that before he paid someone to hack the computer system. Which, by the way, is not only cheating, it's illegal."

"It's illegal." One of the players mimicked her and a bunch of others snickered.

A few of the cheerleaders glared and whispered, and one began laughing a cruel, mocking laugh. Ember's chest tightened. She felt like she had walking into school on the Monday after the Slutkowski Striptease. She glanced over at Charles, who stood kicking at the ground, his expression dark. She wished he would say something, anything.

"Why should we take your word for all this?" Marissa stepped forward. "You've been lying to us since day one."

Ember blinked. She opened her mouth, but no sound came out.

Marissa turned toward the team. "She's a liar and a fake. Her name's not even Ember O'Malley. I figured it out last night and looked her up. Her real name is Emily. She's from New Jersey, and she was a total—"

"Shut up, Marissa. You don't know what you're talking about." Tommy stepped forward. Why was he sticking up for her? And why did he look so nervous? He reached over and grabbed Ember's arm, and that's when things got really crazy.

Charles tackled Tommy to the ground. Schmidt punched the quarterback and told him never to call him an idiot again, at which point several of the other players jumped Schmidt and started screaming at him for ruining their season. Pretty soon the entire team seemed to be punching, kicking, and shouting at each other, and even a couple of cheerleaders joined in the melee.

Ember ducked a stray fist and ran toward the bleachers, followed by Claire.

"Ember, what was Marissa talking about? Why would she say those things?"

Ember turned away. Crap. Claire wanted to believe in her, she could hear it in her voice. How could she tell her it had all been a lie? That their entire friendship had been based on fiction? She took a deep breath and met Claire's gaze. "Things are not always what they seem."

"What the ... What's that supposed to mean?"

Ember hesitated. She wanted to explain, but what good would it do? Eventually, Claire would find out about everything anyway, including the Slutkowski Striptease and her reputation back in Jersey and all the things she foolishly thought she had escaped here. How could she face her once she knew all that? "It means we were never really friends."

"You don't mean that."

"Oh, I do. Believe me. This is the first honest thing I've said to you since we met. We were never really friends, and you're a fool if you think we were."

Claire's eyes filled with tears. "Screw you, Ember O'Malley." She turned and walked away, shouting back over her shoulder. "Or whatever your name is."

Ember slumped down onto the bleachers. She deserved that. Screw her indeed. Screw her fake identity and her so-called life in Boyd County. All she wanted to do was leave, disappear, and she knew just the person who could make that happen.

She pulled out her phone and dialed Deputy Steuben's number. "My cover's been blown."

# CHAPTER THIRTY-EIGHT

The first person Emily saw when she walked into the courtroom was Rosa. The room swirled for a moment, and she grabbed onto her mother's arm for support.

Of course, it wasn't Rosa. It was Rosa's mom. An older but still very beautiful version of her. Emily imagined she would have been even more stunning were it not for the lines of pain etched into her face.

Emily's knees shook as Deputy Steuben led her up the aisle and pointed her toward the witness stand. She'd spent the past four days holed up in a hotel in Newark and the past two hours confined to a tiny office in the courthouse basement waiting to be called by the prosecutor. She wanted to get this over with.

She took the stand and swore to tell the truth. The leather Bible felt smooth and sturdy under her hand, calming her nerves for a moment. As she sat, she saw that Rosa's entire family had come. They filled up four rows of benches—tall, handsome brothers, adorable nieces and nephews, sobbing aunts and grandmothers. Emily's heart pounded in her ears. All of them were relying on her and that inconclusive toxicology report for justice.

She glanced over at the defense table, where Jimmy d'Angelo sat quietly in a dark blue suit, a row of attorneys behind him. He wore a calm but pensive expression. Clearly he'd been coached on how to appear before a jury.

The prosecutor smiled as he approached her. They'd been over this several times in the past two days. It was simple, really. All she had to do was tell the truth.

"You were on the beach the night Rosa Menendez died, is that correct?" he asked.

"Yes."

He took her through a series of questions, asking her what she'd heard and seen, right up through Brad smacking Rosa's drink into the fire. He then presented her with a flask of dark blue liquid. "Is this the color of the drink you saw?"

"It is," she answered.

"Thank you." He turned toward the judge. "Your honor, please let the record show that the liquid she has identified is a concoction of summer ale and Royphnol, commonly known as 'rufies,' or the date rape drug. I have no further questions."

The judge called up the defense attorney for cross-examination. Emily took a deep breath. Here it came. The prosecutor had warned her this could get rough, that the defense's primary goal would be to make her look bad in front of the jury. *I'll do what I can to protect you,* he'd said, *but you need to be prepared to answer some ugly questions.* Emily had a pretty good idea what that meant. She was glad she'd talked her mother into leaving Trina downstairs with one of the deputies.

First, the attorney attacked her testimony, piece by piece. So she was sleeping when Rosa went into the water? And she herself had been drinking? She hadn't actually seen anyone put anything in Rosa's drink, had she? In fact, she wasn't even sure where Rosa had gotten her drink, was she? And how could she be sure about the bluish color in the light of the bonfire? Finally, wasn't it true that she had actually witnessed Jimmy trying to save the victim—performing CPR on her? By the time he'd finished, Emily almost doubted her own testimony.

The defense attorney paused and walked over to his table. He shuffled through some papers. Was he finished? Would he let her go without asking those ugly questions?

He cleared his throat and pointed to a flat-screen off to the side of the witness stand. "Ladies and gentlemen of the jury, Ms. Slovkowski, if you'll direct your attention toward the screen, I have a brief video I'd like to show you."

"Objection." The prosecutor stood. "This has no bearing on the case."

"Your honor, the video speaks to the witness's credibility and motivation for testifying."

Emily's breathing grew shallow. Video? As in, the Slutkowski Striptease? It had to be. She met her mother's eyes. Oh, no. No no no no. Not with her mother sitting here.

The judge called both attorneys to the bar, where they spoke in hushed tones. The next thing she knew, the attorney was pointing a remote at the screen, and there she was, big as life, bikini top in hand. At least they'd had the decency to put a big black bar over her chest. To Emily's horror, the video was more than just the GIF. It went on and on for what seemed like forever—her waving and making kissy faces at the camera and, ugh, letting the guys in the hot tub put their hands all over her. She had never seen the full clip.

As the freak show came to an end, silence enveloped the courtroom. She avoided her mother's eyes, the jurors' eyes, pretty much everyone's eyes. She stared at the railing in front of her, a dark cherry probably, or maybe mahogany. She blinked hard. She would not cry. She wouldn't give Jimmy d'Angelo the satisfaction.

"Ms. Slovkowski." Jimmy's attorney assumed a pitying tone. "I understand this video was filmed over a year ago, is that correct?"

"Yes, sir." Her voice was barely a whisper.

"And do you recall who filmed it?"

Did she recall? He asked the question as breezily as though he were asking if she recalled what she ate for breakfast that morning. She raised her eyes and met Jimmy's level gaze. For a moment, she fantasized about standing and pointing and dramatically shouting out: "He filmed it! He's the person who ruined my life!" But of course, that would play right into their hands. Not to mention, it would be ridiculous.

"Jimmy," she said.

"James d'Angelo, the defendant," the lawyer confirmed. "And isn't it true that this video has caused considerable damage to your reputation, and that you have wanted to get back at the defendant ever since its creation?"

She shook her head. "No. I mean, yes, it hurt my reputation, but this isn't about getting back at him."

"I see." The attorney walked toward her. "In your statement to the police, you indicated you believed you had been drugged in this video, is that correct?"

"Yes."

"You were drinking?"

"Yes."

"Do you have any proof that you were drugged, or do you just believe you were drugged?"

"I know I was. Just like Rosa."

"I see. Just like Rosa. Of course, we have no proof that Rosa was drugged, and you have no proof that you were drugged. But you *believe* you were. Wouldn't that be a convenient way to explain your behavior? Isn't it possible, Ms. Slovkowski, that you imagined the discoloration of Rosa's beer? That your allegations are in fact based on your desire to find an excuse for what took place that night in this video?"

Emily closed her eyes. What if he was right? What if she'd imagined it? What if it was all some fantasy in her head to make Jimmy the bad guy? No, she knew what she saw. She opened her eyes, sat up straight, and said in a loud, clear voice, "No. I didn't imagine anything. I'm confident Rosa was drugged."

The attorney assumed the most condescending smile known to mankind. "Thank you, Ms. Slovkowski. No further questions."

As Emily climbed off the witness stand, a bit dazed and thoroughly humiliated, the attorneys and judge discussed their next move. The prosecutor suggested a lunch break before calling his final witness.

Break or not, Emily was ready to get out of there. She sat down stiffly beside her mother, still unable to look her in the eye. What must she think of her? Emily stared straight ahead at the judge. *Please dismiss us for lunch. Put me out of my misery.* As she pled silently for an escape, her mom's arm settled around her shoulder.

"I'm so proud of you."

Emily melted into her mother's side, and the tears she'd held back during her testimony surfaced. Her mom believed her. And was proud of her. At that moment, she didn't care what anyone else in the whole stupid courtroom thought.

The judge called for a lunch recess. Emily's mom handed her a pack of tissues, and she wiped her eyes. She had skipped breakfast—no way could she eat anything this morning—and was suddenly starving. She kissed her mom on the cheek. "Let's go get Trina and hit the café."

She, her mom, and Deputy Steuben rode the elevator downstairs, and as they stepped off, a cute boy boarded. As the doors closed, he turned to look at her, his eyes widening in recognition.

Zach?

# CHAPTER THIRTY-NINE

Emily had never seen Zach in a suit, with his hair pulled back like that. What was he doing here? She took off toward the staircase.

"Emily!" her mom called after her, but she ignored her.

She tore up the steps, Deputy Steuben close behind, shouting for her to stop. She had to see him. And she could tell by the look in his eyes he was excited to see her, too.

"Zach!" She caught him as he stepped off the elevator.

He smiled, a huge, sexy Zach smile. "Hey, Em." He grabbed her and hugged her, lifting her off the ground and spinning her around.

She buried her face into his neck, breathing him in. How she'd missed his beachy scent.

He pulled away. "I like the red." He ran his fingers lightly through her hair and around her ear, giving her earlobe a light tug. "I missed you."

"Me too." She kissed him. It was a light kiss, quick and sweet and … awkward? It had a weird vibe, or was that her imagination? Emily pushed away the thought. She was being silly. Anyway, they were standing in the middle of the crowded courthouse hallway with Deputy Steuben looming four feet away. A little awkwardness might be expected. "What … what are you doing here?"

Zach looked down at his feet. "Same as you, I guess."

"Same as me? You mean, you're a witness?"

He pulled out his phone and checked the time. "I need to run. Cool seeing you again." And with that, he took off.

Emily's stomach twisted. *Cool seeing you again?* She turned to Deputy Steuben. "He's a witness? On which side?"

Deputy Steuben cursed under his breath. "Let's go back downstairs. Your mother and sister are waiting."

"Tell me."

He sighed and pressed the elevator down button.

"He's a witness for the prosecution, same as you, but—"

"Oh, thank God." She breathed a sigh of relief. So after all of his protests for her to drop it, Zach had decided to testify as well. But what would he say? He didn't know anything about the case, did he? Unless Jimmy had told him something incriminating. Or maybe he was going to be a character witness for her, tell everyone that he knew Emily Slovkowski better than anyone, and he knew she was not the person in that video. "Can I come back and watch?"

"No." Deputy Steuben was emphatic. "You're going to stay downstairs in case you need to be called again." He boarded the elevator and held the door for her. "Come on."

"I know you *want* me to stay downstairs. But do I *have* to? Legally?"

He gave her a pointed stare. "You're holding up the elevator."

"Fine." She got on. "Do I have to?"

Deputy Steuben's jaw tightened as they descended. He watched the numbers at the top of the elevator door. "The judge didn't order witness exclusion, but—"

"So I can come back and watch. Excellent. I'll do that."

Steuben closed his eyes and groaned, but he didn't protest.

\*\*\*

After lunch, Emily and Deputy Steuben slipped into a bench in the back of the courtroom. Her mom stayed downstairs with Trina. As they waited for the judge to return, Emily overheard the man and woman sitting in front of her reviewing the facts of the case. They were young lawyers, or maybe law students.

The woman shook her head and sighed. "All I can say is, this next witness had better be good, or the prosecutor should lose his job for bringing this case to court."

"Lose his job?" The man snorted. "He should be disbarred from ever practicing again. This is an embarrassment. If you look up 'hopeless case' in next year's Law Practice 101 text, I'll bet you find a picture of him and that last witness."

The woman giggled, and Emily gripped the edge of her bench. How dare they? But what if they were right? Did the jury feel that way? Was the case hopeless? For the first time it occurred to her that everything she'd been through and had put her mom and sister through might be for nothing. Jimmy might walk.

At last, the bailiff called the court to order, and Zach took the stand. His testimony started out simply enough. Yes, he was there the night Rosa died. He'd seen Jimmy talking to her before the volleyball game. And yes, he had tried along with Jimmy to perform CPR. Then the prosecutor changed his line of questioning.

"Mr. Reagan, earlier we watched a video of one of your friends, Emily Slovkowski, in a hot tub, a video that was filmed by the defendant. Are you familiar with it?"

Emily's face burned. Did he really have to bring up the striptease again? Wasn't he the one who'd protested earlier that it had no bearing on the case?

Zach answered that he was familiar with the video, and that he was in fact at the party that night.

"Was there anything unusual about Ms. Slovkowski's behavior in that video?" the prosecutor asked.

"Objection!" The defense attorney stood.

"I'll rephrase the question. Based on your interactions with Ms. Slovkowski, were you surprised to see the way she behaved in the video?"

"Yes, I was."

Emily breathed a sigh of relief. So he had been called to be a character witness. He'd agreed to stand up for her before God, the jury, and everyone else in the courtroom.

Only Zach didn't stop there. He stared down at the same railing she'd trained her eyes on a couple of hours earlier and continued, his voice low and shaking. "I mean, I was surprised at first, but later it made sense."

What? Emily's mouth dropped open. The man and woman in front of her looked at each other, eyebrows raised.

"Let's go." Deputy Steuben nudged her to stand, but Emily refused to move. Train wrecks may be horrifying, but you don't take your eyes off them.

The prosecutor urged Zach on. "Tell us what you mean by that."

Zach cleared his throat, still staring at the railing. "I found out a couple of days later that she had been drugged. With Royphnol."

Emily's head began to swim, and her breath grew shallow. He knew? He'd known all this time?

"I see," the prosecutor continued. "Do you know who gave her the Royphnol?"

Zach glanced up ever so briefly in her direction before gluing his eyes once again to the railing. "I did."

The woman in front of Emily gasped, and the courtroom erupted in a cauldron of murmurs. Emily grasped Deputy Steuben's arm. What was he saying?

Zach cleared his throat and looked straight at her. "It was an accident. I swear, I had no idea. It was some stupid joke Jimmy played. He gave me a spiked Jell-O shot and told me to give it to the next hot girl who walked in the door. I didn't know it had a rufie in it until a few days later."

He thought she was hot? Even then? Emily shook her head. She was missing the point here. Zach had drugged her. And maybe it was an accident, but he should have told her sooner. Much, much sooner.

Zach testified that he'd heard Jimmy talk about giving girls rufies a few times since then. He hadn't actually seen him spike Rosa's drink, but he believed it was very possible.

As he climbed down off the stand, Emily rushed out of the courtroom. She needed to be alone, so she headed for the one place Deputy Steuben wouldn't follow her—the women's room.

She leaned against a stall door, shaking. How could he? He knew she'd been drugged. He knew other girls were being drugged, had in fact witnessed the death of one of those girls, yet his reaction until now had been silence. "Let it drop," he'd told her, over and over. Coward. What an idiot he was.

What an idiot she was.

# CHAPTER FORTY

Emily checked the clock beside the bed. It was almost eleven, so why was someone knocking on her hotel room door? Maybe it was her mom. Maybe she and Trina were having as much trouble sleeping next door as she was. She set down her book and swept Oliver off her lap. She peered through the peephole to find Deputy Steuben grinning and practically bouncing up and down in the hallway.

"What's up?"

"Sorry to bother you. I saw that your light was on, and I just had to tell someone … "

"It's fine. Tell me what?"

Steuben grasped both her arms. "I just got the call.

Jimmy confessed. You don't need me anymore."

"He confessed?" Emily beamed. "So what does that mean? Prison? How long?"

"Well, like I said, for starters, it means you're free. No one has any reason to threaten you or Trina anymore. You get your identity back."

"Okay." She guessed she should be excited about that, or happy, or at least relieved, but mostly she felt numb. Getting to be Emily Slovkowski again didn't seem like such a great deal at this point. "What about Jimmy? What'll happen to him?"

Steuben let her go and looked down at his hands. "He turned state's witness against some guys we've been trying to nail for a long time."

"Wait. What? What does that mean exactly?"

"It means he's going to testify against—"

"I understand what state's witness means. You're looking at one, remember? What does it mean for him?"

"Listen, Emily, I—"

"Oh, no. Don't even. If he walks … "

"He won't walk. He'll do some time. At least a few months, and then probation."

"A few months?" And then he'd be out—hanging out on the shore, playing volleyball, going to school, working, dating—like none of this had ever happened.

Emily launched herself at Deputy Steuben. He held her back, but he let her punch at his chest. She was sobbing now, and punching, and sobbing and punching. "How could you let this happen? This was the plan all along, wasn't it? You knew they were going to offer him a deal." She crumpled to the floor, her face buried in her hands. "You know who didn't get a deal? Rosa. Rosa doesn't get to come back after a few months. I'll bet her mom would give anything to have her come back after a few months."

Steuben said nothing for a long time as she sobbed. Finally, he walked into her room, back toward the bathroom, and returned with a tissue box. "If it makes you feel any better, the men he's testifying against are the ones who ran the rufie operation … among many other criminal enterprises. And they should be going away for a long, long time."

She blew her nose. That did make her feel a little better. At least some good would come of all this. "So what now?"

Steuben offered his hand and helped her up. "Get some sleep. In the morning, we'll meet with your mom and figure out what happens next."

Getting some sleep was easier said than done. As Emily fought with her sheets and blankets and tried to get comfortable in a hotel bed that she couldn't seem to get used to, another knock came. This time it was past midnight, and she peered out to find Zach staring through the peephole at her.

Crap. Where was Deputy Steuben? Shouldn't he have intercepted him? Oh, right. She was free of him, which meant he was free of her, too. He was probably down in the hotel lobby bar enjoying a cold one.

She rested her head against the door. "Go away."

"Em, please. We need to talk."

"No, we don't. We really don't."

"Please. Five minutes. That's all I'm asking."

She said nothing for a solid minute. When she looked out again, Zach was still there. He wore a pair of jeans with a hole in the knee and her favorite heather-gray sweatshirt—the one that brought out the blue in his eyes. Double crap. She opened the door and retreated into the room. She sat on the edge of her bed, grabbing a pillow in case she felt like doing some more punching.

Zach stood awkwardly inside the doorway. "What do you want me to say?"

She raised her eyebrows. "You're the one who said we need to talk." No way would she help him out.

"Okay." He took a deep breath. "Let me start with I'm sorry."

Emily crossed her arms in front of her chest. Sorry

for what? Sorry for drugging her? Sorry for lying to her for the past year? Sorry for letting the entire school call her a slut—treat her like a slut—when he knew all along she'd been drugged? Or maybe he was sorry for telling her over and over that she should abandon the case—abandon Rosa.

"You have to understand … I didn't know what would happen to me if I told anyone. I could have gotten in a lot of trouble for giving you that shot."

Ah, so he was sorry for being a coward. Fair enough.

"Could you please say something?"

Emily sighed and threw the pillow aside. She had no desire to punch Zach. If anything, she felt sorry for him. He wasn't a bad person. He was weak. Weak and immature. He went in and out with the waves, never really thinking about anything but the ride, never looking far enough beyond his surfboard to consider the enormity and depth of the ocean.

"I do have one question." She hated how her voice shook. "You and me. Was that you feeling sorry for me? Or guilty?"

"No. No way." Zach sat down next to her and took her hands in his. "That was real. A hundred percent. I loved you, Emily. I still do. And I still want to make this work."

She leaned into his chest and let him put his arms around her as she cried. She didn't realize how badly she'd needed to hear that, how terrified she'd been that their entire relationship had been a sham and that maybe no one ever had or ever would truly love her.

A huge part of her wanted to stay like this forever. She let him stroke her neck and whisper into her hair that everything would be okay, that they'd find a way to get through this, and he'd make everything up to her. For so long, she'd wanted nothing more than to be back in his arms and to get back what they'd had before the night of the bonfire.

Or what she'd thought they had.

She pulled away. "You should go."

"But—"

"Don't." Emily pulled at one of his curls and let it go, watching it bounce back perfectly into place. If only relationships could be like that, could bounce back after being stretched to their limits. But she knew theirs never could, and she wasn't even sure she wanted it to. "It's over, Zach." It was beyond over.

Zach nodded and stood. As he opened the door, she called to him. "Zach?"

He turned.

"Goodbye."

# CHAPTER FORTY-ONE

"You need another smudge over here." Emily dabbed her mascara brush across the left side of Trina's chin and rubbed in the black streak with her thumb. "Perfect. You look like you haven't bathed in weeks."

She and her mom had created "pros" and "cons" lists to decide whether to stay in Jersey or move back to Boyd County. This time, Trina had appeared on only one of the lists. She loved it here. She had lots of friends and was doing great in school, and she'd literally performed cartwheels down the hotel hallway when they told her she'd be back just in time for the opening night of *Annie*.

For Emily, it didn't really matter. It was a lose-lose proposition. There was nothing for her back in Jersey, and there was nothing for her here. Everyone now knew exactly who she was, and not only would she have the honor of being Emily Slutkowski, but she would have the additional distinction of being The Girl Who Ruined the School's Chance to Go to State. Still, at least here she wouldn't need to worry about running into Jimmy d'Angelo. Or Zach.

"We need to get going, girls. Are you ready?" Their mom appeared in the doorway. "You look great! Nice job with the makeup."

"Two minutes," Emily promised. She grabbed a comb and began teasing Trina's hair. "You need more volume."

"Em?" Trina looked up at her sister, her face serious.

"Yeah?"

"Are you glad to be back?"

Emily shrugged. "Sure. It'll be great."

It would be horrible. She dreaded seeing her former friends. Claire had texted her a few times while she was in Jersey, asking her to call so they could talk, but she'd ignored her. Charles hadn't communicated with her at all, not a single text, and she'd tried to ignore that fact as well. She went through the whole ostracism thing a year ago; she could deal with it again now.

It wasn't until Trina wiped away the tear on Emily's

cheek that she realized she was crying.

"Everything will be okay," Trina said. "You'll see."

Emily nodded and sniffed.

"The sun will—"

"Oh, don't even." Emily tickled her sister until she squealed for her to stop. When their mother reappeared, tapping at her watch, they both hooted and raced outside to the car, calling for shotgun.

***

Emily wore a black hoodie with the hood up and slouched low in her auditorium seat. Her sister's name was printed in the program, so the entire town would surely be on the lookout for her. Boyd County didn't have many scandals, and she had no doubt they made the most of the ones that did come along.

Of course, she'd have to face everyone eventually, but her mom and Principal Keane had set her up to get through Christmas break and midterms at home. She hoped to put off seeing her classmates as long as possible.

She snuck out to use the restroom during the last song before intermission. She wanted to get in and out before the crowds, but when she opened the bathroom door, she ran into someone.

"Ember?" It was Sarah. Crap.

"Um. Hi. It's Emily now." She lowered her head and tried to slip around her, but Sarah didn't move.

"You're back."

"Yep." Thanks, Captain Obvious.

"How are you? I was worried about you."

Worried? Had Sarah somehow missed the newsflash that Emily had ruined everything for the school? "I'm okay, I guess. How about you? How's *Grease* going? It opens tomorrow, right?"

"Yeah, tomorrow night. I'm hoping we'll be ready for it. It's been extra crazy because of … well, you know. Never mind."

"Never mind what?"

"Oh, nothing." Sarah looked away. "It's just that tech crew has been pretty screwed up ever since … "

Of course. She hadn't even considered that. Tommy was no doubt suspended, or maybe even expelled. So not only did she ruin the football season, but she also messed up *Grease*. Wonderful. One more reason for Claire and everyone else to hate her.

"You'll be there, right? You have to come see it."

Emily shook her head and scooted by her toward the nearest stall. "Probably not a good idea. But good luck. I mean, break a leg. I'm sure you'll do great."

# CHAPTER FORTY-TWO

For the second night in a row, Emily hid in the cover of a darkened auditorium. She'd decided to check out *Grease* after all, though she'd slipped in late and planned to leave early. And this time she'd made sure to go to the bathroom before she left the house.

Aside from the occasional misplaced spotlight, the show was fantastic. The chemistry between Claire and Ryan almost made her forget that she was watching a play, that Sandy and Danny were fictional characters, and that being in love pretty much sucked.

Emily lost herself in the story so thoroughly she forgot to leave before it ended. It wasn't until the cast began taking their curtain calls that she realized she needed to get out of there. She slipped through a side door and down a darkened hallway, but when she reached the end, the exit door was locked. What the... Wasn't that some sort of fire code violation? As she made her way back, she could hear the crowd emptying out into the auditorium lobby.

Great. Now she was trapped. She'd either have to walk through throngs of people or wait them out. She slouched against a wall. No way could she show her face.

About twenty minutes later, with the crowd noise reduced to a light murmur, Emily decided to make her move. If she wore her hood, kept her head down, and walked quickly, she might be able to sneak out and dash across the parking lot to her car without anyone recognizing her. But as she stood and made her move toward the lobby, she heard voices approaching. Marissa and some other cheerleaders.

Her breath caught. What now? The only thing worse than running into a bunch of her old friends would be for them to discover her lurking here in the shadows. She scurried back down the hallway toward a door on the right-hand side. She wanted to disappear into an office or a closet for a few minutes.

Except when she opened the door, instead of a darkened room, she found herself blinking under the glare of bright fluorescent lights.

"Ember!"

She was in a backstage room, face-to-face with Ryan.

She held her finger up to her lips, her eyes still adjusting. "Shh. Please. No one else can know I'm here." She scanned the room, her gaze falling on a heavy cherry-colored curtain hanging nearby. "Great job tonight, by the way." She headed toward the curtain.

"Ember, wait!"

"Quiet!" She slipped behind it and stepped on someone's foot.

"Ouch!" It was Claire, and her face was the same shade as the curtain.

"Hey, what are you doing? Ohh." Emily grinned, forgetting for a moment that running into Claire was precisely what she'd hoped to avoid.

The two of them disentangled themselves from the curtain and stepped back out into the room. Ryan wore a sheepish expression that left no doubt as to what she had interrupted when she came bursting in.

Emily and Claire stood facing each other. Well, this was awkward. On many levels.

"How about I meet you out by the soda machines?" Ryan asked.

Claire nodded and waved him away without ever

taking her eyes off Emily. "So the rumors are true. You're back." Her tone was measured. Did she mean that in a good way or in a Screw-You-Ember-O'Malley-Or-Whatever-Your-Name-Is way?

"Listen, Claire, I don't know how much you know about what—"

"Pretty much all of it."

"Right." Emily's face burned, and she turned away. Of course, she would. The trial had been plastered on the news for the entire week back in Jersey. Even the striptease video had somehow been leaked online. At this point, everyone in Boyd County had surely seen and read every humiliating detail. "I don't blame you if you think the worst of me. I'm not who I said I was. I kind of wanted to be, but I'm not. I'm Emily Slovkowski, better known as Emily Slutkowski, from the Jersey Shore. I've never even been to Philadelphia, though I have visited New York a couple of times, and I actually am hoping to go to Long Island U for photography, but I never—"

"Emily." Claire interrupted, her eyes guarded, stony. "None of that is the point. I mean, I get it. You were in Witness Protection. You had to lie. And as far as the whole 'Slutkowski' thing goes, that's craziness. You were drugged, right? Even if you hadn't been, why should you take the rap when every single idiot guy in that tub stood there and cheered you on? Not to mention the loser who taped it."

Emily tried to speak but couldn't. Her mouth opened and closed like a fish washed onto shore, dazed and confused outside of its element. Claire didn't see her as a slut. She saw her as someone who had been wronged. Somewhere deep inside, she knew Claire was right, had always known it, but she hadn't allowed herself to believe it. Instead, she'd worn the scarlet "S" and done her best to become the girl in the video.

Why hadn't she fought it? Claire would have fought it. Emily sat down on a nearby step stool as a year's worth of tears spilled out—part shock at Claire's reaction, part relief at finding someone who finally understood, and part mourning over a miserable, wasted year. She buried her face in her hands and sobbed.

When Claire pulled up a stool next to her and placed her arms around her shoulders, she leaned into her. What had she done to deserve a friend like Claire? She pulled away, choking through her sobs. "So what is the point?"

"What?"

"You said the lying and the video weren't the point. Which means there is a point. What is it?"

Claire sighed. "When you said I was a fool to ever

think we were friends—"

"I just meant that—"

"I know what you meant. But how could you believe that? How could you think I was only friends with you because you were from Philadelphia, or because of some stupid made-up past?"

"It wasn't so much my past, it was … me. I wasn't who I pretended to be. Trust me, I'm not the Ember O'Malley you think you know."

Claire raised her eyebrows. "So that was all an act? You're not actually smart, funny, sweet, and brave? Well, then you deserve an Academy Award. You really should try out for the spring musical."

Emily gave a weak smile and wiped her tears. "You really think I'm brave?"

"Are you kidding me? The way you stood up to the whole football team? Not to mention, testifying in a murder trial? Yes, I think you're brave. In fact, you're the one who inspired me."

"Inspired you?"

"To ask Ryan out. I figured if you could risk your life like that, the least I could do was risk a little heartache."

Emily gave Claire a fist bump. "I'm so proud of you. Speaking of which … your throat must be parched after all that singing. You should head on over to the soda machines and get a drink."

Claire grinned. "Pretty cool, huh?"

"Very cool. You two are adorable together."

They gave each other a long hug, and Emily slipped back out and down the hallway. As she made her way outside to her car, she felt herself breathing easier than she had in days. Claire still wanted to be friends. She couldn't ask for anything more.

Well, maybe one thing more.

# CHAPTER FORTY-THREE

Emily ran her fingers along the rough wall of the bridge, closing her eyes as she relived her kiss with Charles. The sense of freedom and simplicity and … oh, yeah, the hotness. She sighed and debated texting him—something she'd thought about a million times in the ten days since she'd returned to Boyd County. She'd even composed a few texts, but she could never bring herself to hit "send."

She leaned against the wall and breathed in the smell of pine. It was so quiet and peaceful here. She'd come every day since she'd returned, always during school hours so she wouldn't have to worry about running into anyone. Now she had an entire portfolio of bridge photos, taken on bright days and cloudy days, from inside and outside, and from every angle. She'd even climbed a nearby tree and taken a bunch of shots from above.

Today, though, was special. Today it had snowed— only about an inch, but it was enough to transform the bridge into a magical scene from a Christmas card. She half expected to hear sleigh bells and see a horse-drawn carriage trundle through.

She unzipped her camera case. The pink candy heart still sat at the bottom. She'd grown so used to seeing it there, she almost overlooked it now. Almost. She adjusted the focus on her lens and peered through her viewfinder at the hole in the wall. She loved the way it formed a natural frame for the view outside, and today that view was spectacular. The creek was partly frozen, and snow-covered icicles clung to the rocks. As she played with different focus settings, she realized the snow had begun to fall again.

She sighed. She should probably go. Her mother had protested when she'd grabbed the keys this morning. She didn't like Emily driving in the snow, and now she'd be really worried. On the other hand, it couldn't hurt to stay for just a few more minutes. She'd love to get some shots of the swirling flakes. She leaned out of the hole and zoomed out for a wide shot of the creek, the banks, and the surrounding landscape.

Wait. Whose car was that parked behind hers?

"Well, look who it is."

Emily's heart pounded as she turned to find Schmidt's massive figure looming at the entrance.

"If you want to jump, I'll be happy to push you." He stepped toward her, and the old wooden planks groaned beneath his weight. As he came closer, she could see the rancor in his eyes. Why wasn't he in school? Christmas break didn't start for two more days.

She shivered. Of course. He'd been expelled or suspended. Because of her.

"Hello, Marcus." Her voice sounded calmer than she felt. "It was poison, you know."

"What?"

"Romeo and Juliet. Cyanide, most likely, though Shakespeare never actually—"

"Shut up." Schmidt closed the distance between them. "You act like you're so much better than me, but I saw that video. Everyone saw it. You're a low-life Jersey Shore whore. Admit it."

Emily's face burned. "I was drugged."

"So? Drugs might make you slur your words or say stupid stuff, but I've never heard of them making girls strip in front of a whole room full of guys." Schmidt leaned in, his face just a few inches from hers. "You wanted to do that, and you know it."

She glanced beyond him toward the path outside. She'd seen Schmidt on the football field. For a big guy, he was quick. Even if she could slip past him, she doubted she could outrun him all the way to her car. She clutched her camera, ready to swing it if he tried anything. "You don't know the first thing about me. Much less what I want." She knew she was practically daring him to do something stupid, but she didn't care. She was sick of guys making assumptions about her because of one stupid video.

To her surprise, Schmidt reached down and grabbed her camera. He wrested it away from her and dangled it by its strap out the hole in the wall. "I know you want your camera back."

She blinked. Maybe he didn't plan to hurt her. Maybe he just wanted to harass her, payback for getting him in trouble.

Schmidt swung the camera wildly above the ice. Condensation was beginning to collect on its lens.

Emily forced a smile. "Tell you what. You give my camera back, and I'll do something for you."

"What did you have in mind?" He leered at her suggestively.

She narrowed her eyes. "Not that. Believe me." She sweetened her tone. "How about I refrain from posting a rather … shall we say … embarrassing photo I took of you the last time we were here at the bridge?"

"What photo?" Schmidt stopped swinging the camera.

"You don't remember?"

He furrowed his brow and tilted his head as if concentrating. "No. I mean, I was pretty wasted. Not that it matters. Everybody knows I get crazy when I'm drunk. Go ahead and post it."

Emily shrugged. "Fine. I'd call this more humiliating than crazy, but if you're okay with it … "

"What was it? Was I peeing in the creek? Because everyone's seen me do that before."

"Um. No." Emily grimaced. "But thanks for the visual."

"What then?"

"You'll see. Don't worry about it. We all make mistakes, right?"

"Tell me." Schmidt's expression morphed from defiant to worried.

Emily paused as if considering his request. She held out her hand. "First, give me the camera."

Schmidt straightened his arm, holding the camera out further. He let go of the strap one finger at a time until he was holding it between only his thumb and forefinger. He began swinging it again.

Emily held her breath and gave what she hoped came off as a carefree shrug. "Fine. Your funeral."

She turned to go.

"Wait. Tell me."

"Not unless you give me the camera."

Schmidt glared, but he reeled the camera in and held it out to her.

"Thank you." Emily grabbed it and forced herself to walk slowly, a casual saunter, toward the entrance. "That was smart of you."

"So what was the picture?"

Emily kept walking. When she reached the entrance, she turned. "What picture? I didn't bring my camera. Don't you know, cameras and partying don't mix?"

She turned and ran to her car, hopped in, and skidded away. Schmidt followed close behind, yelling and cursing. He threw a snowball that nearly took out her back window. Not bad for a defensive guy.

Emily took a deep breath as she pulled onto the main road. It was snowing harder now, making it more difficult to distinguish the pavement from the flat land surrounding it. What an idiot Schmidt was. Still, one phrase echoed in her ears over and over: *low-life Jersey Shore whore*.

Did everyone here think of her that way? Did Charles?

Maybe it was the adrenaline, maybe she was feeling especially bold after her encounter with Schmidt, or maybe it was simply the fact that Charles's house was nearby and her car was skidding wildly in the snow, but she did something she should have done ten days ago. She pulled over and texted him. "Meet me at the barn."

# CHAPTER FORTY-FOUR

Emily awoke with a start, bumping her head against the metal railing of the loft. It took her a moment to realize where she was. She'd fallen asleep waiting for Charles. How long had she been there? Where was he?

She checked her phone. The only text was a quick "Thx and be careful" from her mom. Emily had sent her a message earlier to let her know she was waiting out the storm at a friend's house. It was after four o'clock. School should have let out more than an hour ago. There would be no *Bulletin* this week because of the holiday, so Charles should have been home by now.

A knot formed in her stomach. He wasn't coming.

She'd finally gotten up the nerve to contact him, and he was ignoring her. Now what? She could walk down the lane to his house, but if he didn't want to see her, what was the point? She sat up and brushed the hay from her jeans. Perhaps the snow had stopped. As she headed toward the staircase, she heard something. The door. A rush of cold air swirled up toward her as it opened.

She peered over the railing to find Charles stomping his boots on the hard concrete and shaking snow off his coat.

He glanced up, and she caught her breath. She'd almost forgotten the intensity of his eyes. He said nothing as he crossed the barn floor and slowly climbed the stairs. With each step he took, Emily grew more nervous. She'd worried so much about whether he would show up, she hadn't thought about what to say when he got here.

When he reached the loft, he sat down next to her, his expression as cold as the snow still flaking off his coat.

"You made it."

"This *is* my barn."

"Right. I just meant … I was worried."

"The roads are a mess."

Of course. "Thanks for coming."

"Like I said, it's my barn."

Emily shrank away from his harsh tone. Tears

sprang to her eyes, but she blinked them away. He wanted nothing to do with her now, that was clear, but she had to tell him her side of things. It may not change his opinion, but she needed him to know. She took a deep breath. "So about the video. Not something you expected to see, I'm sure. Not the person you thought you knew, and—"

"What are you talking about?"

"The … you mean, you haven't seen it?"

"No, of course I've … " Charles's face turned as red as the outside of the barn. "I mean, I know about the video. Because it's out there, and you're in it, and so … yes, I've seen it. But that has nothing to do with anything."

Emily shrank into herself. Great. Now he was thinking about the video. She wished she could crawl beneath the hay and disappear.

Charles kicked the railing, sending a loud metallic clang echoing through the barn, but when he spoke again, his voice had lost its edge. "Listen, Em, I honest to God don't care about that. It was more than a year ago. Those losers drugged you. And if you look into your eyes, you can see it's not you, not really."

Emily smiled despite herself. "You noticed my eyes?"

Charles blushed again and laughed. "That might

have been on the second viewing. Which, by the way, was also the last."

They sat in silence for a moment. Finally, she asked him, "So if it's not about the video, then what? Because clearly you're angry with me about something."

He grabbed a piece of hay and twirled it between his fingers. "Why did you come here?"

Emily shrugged. "Mainly because of my sister. There's really nothing left for us back in—"

"No, I mean, why did you come *here*? To the barn? You haven't said a word to me since, you know … "

That day on the bridge. Was that it? He thought the kiss—that wonderful, incredible, beautiful kiss—had somehow messed things up between them? Oh, man. "I came here because … " She reached over and clasped his hand to stop the twirling. "Because I missed you. And I needed to know what you thought about all of this. Because I couldn't bear it if you thought of me the way everyone else does."

"What do you mean, the way everyone else does?"

"As … you know." She pulled her hand away and imitated Schmidt's drawl. "A low-life Jersey Shore whore."

"What? What are you talking about? Of course I don't think of you that way. Nobody thinks of you that way."

"Oh, some people think of me that way. Trust me."

"Well, those people are stupid. You should ignore them." He started again with the twirling. "If you missed me so much, why haven't you texted or called? Why did you blow me off for two days and then leave without saying goodbye? And why the hell didn't you come to me when you figured out what was going on with the hacking? That was *our* story, you know."

Emily blinked, her thoughts reeling. "Why do you think? I knew as soon as I outed Tommy my cover would be blown. You'd know everything, and I couldn't deal with that. Which is also why I haven't texted or called. I had no idea how you'd react."

"So you decided to shut me out altogether? Because that's so much better than giving me a chance."

She closed her eyes. She'd been so worried for so long about what Charles would think if he knew the truth, she hadn't considered the possibility that she might be hurting him. "I'm sorry. This whole thing has been really hard, you know? A lot to handle. And now to come back and face everyone … "

Charles finally dropped the piece of hay, and he took her hands in his. "I know. The thing is, you don't need to handle it alone. I'll help, but you need to let me."

Emily leaned into him. "What about the fact that I screwed up the football championship? Does everyone hate me for that? Do *you* hate me for that? Even a little?"

Charles grimaced. "Okay, I'm not gonna lie. Some people do hate you for that. But I repeat: those people are stupid and should be ignored. If we can't win fair, what's the point of winning?" He narrowed his eyes. "You did set off quite a brawl, though. Do you realize I spent a week in detention for jumping Tommy?"

She couldn't help but smile. "That was a pretty good tackle for a kicker," she teased. "Though I don't think it was necessary. For some reason, he seemed to be trying to help me, but I have no idea why."

"I do," Charles said. "Believe me, we went over it a million times in Principal Keane's office."

"Really? So, why? I've been trying to figure it out for the past three weeks."

Charles reached over and plucked a piece of hay out of her hair. "After you caught Tommy and Coach under the bridge, he started looking for something on you. Of course, the Marshals didn't make that easy. They had pretty much wiped you off the Internet."

"But with his hacking skills … "

"Exactly. He found some pictures of you and the video and figured out basically who you were, but he didn't know you were in Witness Protection until later. Once he figured that part out, he didn't really want to out you. I mean, it's one thing to blow someone's cover if you think they're trying to escape an embarrassing video; it's another when you realize they're running from the Mob."

Emily nodded. Mystery solved. "Of course, he didn't tell me that since he needed me to keep my mouth shut."

"Right." Charles put his arm around her waist. "It was brave of you to speak up. Especially knowing he could blow your cover."

There was that word again. *Brave*. Emily shrugged. "I knew I had to head back to Jersey for the trial soon anyway. I didn't have much to lose. Well, except for you. Which did scare me."

Charles pulled her into him and kissed her. A long, sweet kiss.

He still wanted to be with her. Even after everything. She knew now she should have trusted him, should have told him sooner about the—

She pulled away and leaned her head into his chest. Tears filled her eyes as she breathed in the smell of his leather coat. "There's more to it."

He stroked her hair. "More to what?"

She sat up and scooted away from him. "More to … my past. More than the video."

A shadow crossed over Charles's face. "What do

you mean?"

She pulled her legs up and wrapped her arms around her knees. He didn't need to know about all the guys she'd messed around with, but she needed to tell him. How else could she face him? How else could she kiss him? She buried her head into her knees. "After the video got out, people made a lot of assumptions about me. Guys. They had certain expectations, and I … well, I did my best to live up to those expectations."

Charles said nothing. For a long time, they sat in silence except for her soft sobs.

"What must you think of me?" she asked. "What kind of girl do you think I am?"

Charles placed his hand under her chin and slowly lifted her head until her eyes met his. "What kind of girl do I think you are? I think you're the kind of girl who would crawl under a tractor to save a tiny kitten. I think you're the kind of girl who would move to the middle of nowhere to protect her sister. I think you're the kind of girl who would risk everything to tell the truth for the sake of some girl she didn't even know."

Emily reached up and touched his lips, struggling to believe the words that were coming out of them. Is that how he saw her? Even knowing about her past? "I don't deserve you," she said finally.

"Of course you do. You deserve better, probably,

but lucky for me, the competition in Boyd County is pretty slim."

She laughed. "I'm pretty sure you're the only nerdy, strip-dancing, football-superhero, pirate-loving cowboy. Which works for me."

He rolled his eyes. "I told you, I'm no cowboy."

"But you don't deny the nerdy, strip-dancing, football-superhero, pirate-loving parts?"

He shrugged, a smile tugging at his lips. "I'm not much for labels, but if you insist." He leaned over and kissed her again, a strong, slow, honest kiss. "Thank you for telling me everything. It means a lot. I finally feel like I'm unraveling the mystery that is Emily Slovkowski."

"I'm not such a mystery," she said. "Not really."

"Well, you have been to me. Right down to your tan lines, which apparently were created by this tiny mermaid." He reached up and stroked her ear cuff.

Emily blushed. She'd forgotten she'd put it on before she left the house.

"So what's the story with this?"

"Nothing," she said. "It's part of who I used to be. Who I am."

Charles kissed her ear, the tip of her nose, her lips. "Then I like it. I like everything about it."

# ACKNOWLEDGEMENTS

Writing often is seen as a solitary pursuit, but my writing, at least, is supported by so many. I owe you all a debt of gratitude.

To the Swoon Romance team—with special thanks to Georgia McBride—for taking a chance on a new writer and making my books a reality.

To my agent, Andrea Somberg, who somehow manages to keep the waiting (which is of course the hardest part) to a minimum.

To Ellen Braaf, for always giving so generously of her time and her encouragement.

To Kathy Chappell, whose questions make me see my stories in new ways.

To the Cudas—Lisa Amowitz, Heidi Ayarbe, Pippa Bayliss, Dhonielle Clayton, Trish Eklund, Lindsay Eland, Cathy Giordiano, Cyndy Henzel, Christine Faul Johnson, and Kate Milford. You are my tribe.

To the Writer's Center, with special thanks to my fellow WC-Leesburg Committee members, Brash, Ellen Braaf, Louise Baxter, Brad Holzwart, Jeff Kleinman, Jennifer March, and Val Patterson.

To fellow writers Tom Angleberger, Erica Chapman, and Noreen Wald.

To my many friends in the SCBWI Mid-Atlantic Chapter, the Blue Boards, the Virginia Chapter of Romance Writers of America, and the Young Adult Chapter of Romance Writers of America.

To my college roommate Karen Folco, who will never let me forget it if I don't acknowledge her.

To the LifeSigns Youth, with a special shout out to Claire G. and Emily J., who helped inspire one of my favorite lines in the book.

To my parents, Bea and Ted Acorn, and my siblings, Deb Acorn, Karen Benfield, and Ted Acorn, whose unending support means so much.

To Eris and Sarah, who are too far away but remain close in my thoughts.

To Joe, always to Joe.

And to God, in whom all things are possible.

## LINDA BUDZINSKI

Linda Budzinski lives in Northern Virginia with her husband, Joe, and their feisty chihuahua, Demitria. She has two step-daughters, Eris and Sarah. She grew up in a tiny town in southeastern Pennsylvania called West Grove, and in the second grade decided she wanted to be a "Paperback Writer," just like in the Beatles song. She majored in journalism in college and now works in nonprofit marketing and communications. She's a sucker for romance and reality TV and has been known to turn off her phone's ringer when watching "The Bachelor." Her favorite flower is the daisy, her favorite food is chocolate, and her favorite song is "Amazing Grace." Her first novel, THE FUNERAL SINGER, was released in September 2013 by Swoon Romance YA.

# OTHER GMMG TITLES YOU MIGHT LIKE

THE FUNERAL SINGER
LIFE IN THE NO-DATING ZONE
RIVAL DREAMS
LOUDER THAN WORDS

Find more awesome teen romance books at
http://www.myswoonromance.com/

Connect with Swoon Romance online:

Facebook: www.Facebook.com/swoonromance
Twitter: https://twitter.com/SwoonRomance
You Tube: www.youtube.com/SwoonRomance
Blog: www.month9booksblog.com
Instagram: https://instagram.com/swoonromance
Request review copies via swoonromancepr@gmail.com

# THE
# Funeral Singer
## LINDA BUDZINSKI

# LIFE in the
## no-dating ZONE

Patricia B. Tighe

# NATALIE DECKER

# Rival Dreams

## Their Rules. Game On.

# LOUDER THAN WORDS

A NOVEL

# WORDS

TO FIND HER VOICE SHE'LL HAVE TO TRUST HER HEART.

# IRIS ST. CLAIR

A Swoon Romance

CPSIA information can be obtained
at www.ICGtesting.com
Printed in the USA
BVOW08s0825270817
493130BV00001B/8/P

9 781942 664628